To NICOLA

Wrath of the Land

ENJOY!
(BEWARE THE SEWERS...)

Wrath of the Land

By

Oli Jacobs

Cover art by Elaine M Will

Website: http://www.cuckoosnestpress.com

Social Media: @ElaineMWill (Twitter), @elaine.m.will (Instagram)

Proofing services provided by Marc Paterson

Website: http://marcpaterson.contently.com

Social Media: @marcpaters0n (Twitter)

To those that follow...

...And to those that lead.

Also by Oli Jacobs

Bad Sandwich
The Children of Little Thwopping
The Station 17 Chronicles
Wilthaven
Deep Down There

1

It began, as these things tend to do, with a blocked toilet in West Crumb.

Said toilet – belonging to a Mr and Mrs Wallace of Corbin Hill – had been sluggish for a few weeks now. However, on this occasion, its contents had backed up to such a degree that upon another everyday flush the water rose instead of sank, and quickly threatened to breach the sanctity of the toilets rim.

This had not been an uncommon occurrence in West Crumb of late.

As well as toilets blocking, sinks, drains, and various other outlets linked to the sewage system had begun to spew forth its contents for the surface to see. One expulsion had resulted in a steady stream of faecal produce flowing down West Crumb's High Street, with local teenagers taking great pleasure in the "River of Shit".

Council officials were less amused.

In fact, this stream of disdain found itself pooling on the desk of Ronald Pile, a low level civil servant who had been tasked with assisting the waste department at Crumb County Council. Before now, the most important thing he had managed was the cleaning of the streets and clearing of rogue foliage. With West Crumb's new landmarks – which soon included a fountain of particularly stagnant water – it was now his responsibility to resolve this unsightly issue.

And so, with great aggravation, he set about planning to.

-

Meanwhile, in a small flat on Allard Avenue, Laura Bennett was attacking her own lavatorial lake with an old wire coat hanger. The contents were best left unsaid, but despite destruction by a thousand sharp pokes, the water level had not shifted a millimetre. The only difference from before was that the water now had a delightful brown hue masking the foulness below.

Laura knew she wasn't alone. The other residents in the complex had made similar grumbles over the weeks, and until now she had felt quite lucky in not suffering the disgusting fate. Such hubris had lead to this unholy moment, and her laments were met with empathy by her peers, but not without a knowing smirk.

As a local student, she had not been the most hygienic, this she would freely admit. If it fitted in the toilet, then down it would go. Everything was forgotten with a quick flush. Laura had found the habits of fellow residents to be equally as repugnant, if not worse. Once, she swore she saw a young fellow shove several rolls of kitchen roll down a nearby drain. When asked why, his answer was simple in its absurdity.

"Experiment."

-

It had taken many calls and a few small favours, but Ronald had managed to convince a small cleaning crew to venture down to where he had identified was the central source of the blockage. Under the High Street, an exceptional pooling of filth-rich water had created a whole new ecosystem of waste that was far more intensive than anywhere else in West Crumb. After an on-going chorus of complaint from local businesses, it was here that Ronald had determined action needed to be taken.

A drainage hatch gave the team access into the bowels of the High Street, but upon reaching an entrance to the inner sanctum, they found their way blocked from the inside. Another plan of action was determined, with the cleaners enjoying a soggy wade through a mile of tunnels west of the High Street.

As Ronald sat in the relatively clean sanctuary of his office, a call came through.

"You're through to Pile."

There was a small snigger at the other end, but Ronald had grown to accept this. He was an important man, and had decided long ago to answer in an important manner.

"If you've quite finished…" he said.

"Sorry, Mr Pile," the voice on the other end said, belonging to one of the subterranean cleaners. "We've found the cause of your blockage."

"And?"

"And… well… I've never seen anything like it."

"What do you mean?"

"Well, it's a massive blob."

"A massive *what*?"

"A massive blob. Like, made out of tissues and that."

"A…" Ronald sighed and pinched his nose in agitation. "Well just clear it up."

"We can't."

"Why not?"

"It's pretty big."

"How big?"

"Probably about the size of a couple of buses."

With that, Ronald stopped listening, and tried to get his head around the idea of a mound of tissues the size of a bus.

Two buses, in fact.

-

"They call it a 'fatberg'," Joey said.

When it came to the stranger side of life, Joey was always a good source. Laura had met him through her creative writing course, and had decided he would make good friend material when, upon being asked to submit a fantasy story about elves and dragons, he instead wrote about demons orchestrating a suicide bombing on a train.

It hadn't gone down well.

"A fatberg?"

"Yeah. An iceberg, but with fat."

"Makes sense."

The news had come out pretty swiftly, despite the Council's attempts for it not to. The curious nature of the exceptional mass lying under West Crumb had developed through a series of whispers that went from a member of the cleaning crew, to a member of their family, and then the Internet. Each told in confidence to the other, of course.

After that, there was no stopping the flow. Which was rather counter to the situation they all found themselves in now.

The idea of a fatberg was a known phenomenon, and one that had become more public in recent years. They were blamed on build up on non-soluble materials such as tissues, nappies, condoms, and assorted thick liquids such as oil. Instead of oozing through the sewers and finding a new home rupturing the ecological nature of the ocean, it had instead pooled happily in one part, accumulating more mass until it was big enough to cause chaos.

And that chaos had finally arrived in West Crumb.

"So…"

"So?"

"So what are they doing?" Laura said.

"Breaking it down, I guess."

"How?"

"I don't know. Hammers?"

"They're going to smash it apart with hammers?"

"I mean it's an option…"

"And what then? Flush the remains down the toilet again?"

For reasons that she could not correctly ascertain at that time, the presence of the fatberg had triggered something within Laura. She felt a mild rage at the fact that it existed, and it was caused by the apathetic waste disposal of the people around her. She wasn't much of an environmentalist, no matter how many of their group tried to recruit her, but the sickness she felt when thinking of the 'berg?

It didn't sit well.

-

In general, the fatberg wasn't going to sit well with anyone.

Ronald now had the joy of dealing with the dual headaches of sourcing a cleaning crew capable of destroying the fatberg – with its unique aroma being a particularly difficult selling point – and the actual notion of *how* to destroy it.

Not only that, but his seniors were getting very image conscious - the idea of their town having a fatberg?

It wasn't a good look, to say the least.

With problems building much like the oily mass itself, Ronald didn't have time for the numerous calls he was having to field. He needed a secretary, like Bunson had, but wasn't high enough on the totem to get one. As his phone rang for the 8th time that hour – an hour that was only 18 minutes old – his tone betrayed his stress.

"What?"

"Mr Pile?"

"Speaking?"

"Just checking."

"Just… who is this?

"You'll find out soon enough."

With that, the phone went dead.

And promptly flew across the room, propelled by the impotent rage of Ronald Pile.

2

There was no easy way to remove a mass consisting of all sorts of nastiness, especially one that was the size of several buses and weighed twice as much. One could not hope to simply lubricate it and push it out into the sea – it was already oozing slippery juices as it was, to no avail.

This represented an equally large problem for Ronald. His superiors were making constant noise about what was to be done with the fatberg, while those at the other end of the hierarchy were less keen to investigate it. The consistency of the mass was bad enough, but the smell was something else. No matter how many words were created and contextually used by humanity, they could not come close to describing the wretched nasal violation that the fatberg exuded. The mix of gases of questionable naturalness – methane being the most prominent – meant that stepping too close to the fatberg would suffocate a man in seconds.

Not to mention the fate that would befall a smoker in its vicinity.

Blowing up the fatberg was out of the question. Ronald had posited it early on, but the structural damage to not only the sewers, but also West Crumb as a whole, would be catastrophic. And the Council did not have that kind of budget.

Therefore, it was decided by all parties that the only way to get rid of it was to slowly but surely break it down into tiny pieces, and dispose of it elsewhere. It wasn't the most environmentally friendly solution, but it was one that was both cheap and wouldn't result in the High Street being decimated.

One would think with this resolution in mind, Ronald's problems would be over. Alas, once he had negotiated the method of destruction, the timeline of the work, and convinced several cleaning crews to remove the fatberg thanks to a combination of various safety devices and biohazard clothing – as well as bags of cash - there was a whole new issue to face.

The media.

Not only that, but *how* the Council wanted the media to be handled.

To assist with this, Ronald was assigned a Media Advisor by the higher-ups.

Aaron Stone was young, pragmatic and, in Ronald's opinion, spawned by a committee of sociopaths rather than born naturally. Stone's advice of handling the press mostly revolved around "dehumanising" and "misdirection, which made Ronald realise he was going to have a great deal of difficulty adjusting to this new approach.

-

With West Crumb now absorbed in a macabre excitement over their new landmark, Laura found herself confused by the fervour. After all, a disgusting pile of various dispensable horrors did not really equal the likes of the Pyramids or the Louvre. However, given that the closest claim to fame the town had was an ex-student who had played a tertiary character on a popular sitcom, you took what you could get.

The irony was that this celebrated curiosity was, so far, unseen. Instead, it was a mystery lurking below the streets of West Crumb, known only by those who dared to venture underground. At the moment, there were no plans to perform guided tours or interactive events. Instead, people were content to talk about the fatberg, imagine what the fatberg looked like, and have general opinions about the fatberg.

It was exhausting.

Thankfully, Laura's information conduit for the whole filthy mess – Joey – was a good filter for finding out the facts. As they sat in the garden of one of the many chain pubs in the town, she sipped her pint as Joey talked heights, weights, and general dimensions.

"It's not the biggest they've seen," he said.

"Really?"

"There was one down south, size of 6 double-decker buses and nearly 200 tonnes."

"Are you sure?" Laura said. "That sounds absurdly heavy for what's just messed up loo roll."

"And the rest. It's like a grotesque paper mache. Sure, it's just wet tissues, but shove it all together and you've got yourself the equivalent of an arts and crafts boulder."

"That sounds way too fancy for what's essentially a big ball of shit."

"If it was just shit, it would flush."

"Touché."

From where she sat, Laura saw a small group of dishevelled men – more than likely belonging to the local transient community – lurking around a manhole and murmuring between themselves. As Joey quietly continued his research, Laura watched the show continue as the men decided they wanted to see the fatberg, and would use whatever they could to lever open the manhole.

Using a nearby sign, they would have succeeded, if it hadn't been for some community police officers shooing them off. With that particular piece of theatre over, Laura returned her attention to the stirring Joey.

"They reckon it'll be gone in a few months."

"A few months?"

"It's a big piece of crap."

"Literally. But still…"

"It's not like they have gallons of acid to destroy the thing," Joey said." All they've got are little pickaxes and shovels."

20

Laura nodded in thought. That thought being the horrid sympathy she had for the fools who had to head down with their tiny toffee hammers, and start chipping away at the mass.

-

Given the amount of money Ronald had paid said fools, his sympathy was practically non-existent by now.

He was relying on reports from a designated foreman representing the local water service, which informed him of the various slabs and chunks that they had removed so far. While it was slow, progress was being made, and already several kilos of fatberg were now being wheeled away to dispose of elsewhere. According to the whispers, the more they dug, the more stuff they found had been chucked down people's loos.

"A baby?" Ronald said, as Aaron entered the room.

"They found a baby?"

Ronald turned and gave his attention to the peeking Aaron. "A doll, not an actual baby."

"Well, I've heard of stranger things."

"You're about to hear a lot more," Ronald said, turning to look out of his window. He found in times of stress it was good form to take in the view, even though it mainly consisted of thick leaves and the car park.

That way, he didn't have to entertain Aaron's company in his office.

"Mr Pile?" someone else said.

"They found… *how many cotton buds*?" Ronald said into his phone.

"Mr Pile?"

"What?"

Turning round, Ronald saw whom Aaron was escorting. Dressed in casual suits, with ties hanging from their collars in a style that cared not for the idea of a knot, were a very formal looking couple. One a fairly well coiffed woman, the other a fairly tall and robust gentleman.

Both looked around Ronald's domain with amusement.

"Can I help you?"

The woman looked at Ronald and nodded, still looking around with her partner.

"Aaron, who is this?"

"They…"

"Bureau," the man said, not breaking his study of the office.

"Bureau?" Ronald said. "What Bureau?"

"*The* Bureau," the woman said, smiling.

The only Bureau Ronald knew of was based in America, and he didn't think mountains of waste in a small English town was important to their foreign policy. Besides, these two most definitely didn't look or sound American.

Which was actually a relief.

As Ronald tried to take all this in, he was oblivious to the noises being made on the other end of the phone. What began as confused comments had now evolved into full-blown shouting and hollering. After drawing his attention away from the new wave of intruders he had to deal with, Ronald barked back down the phone.

"What's going on?"

"Wait a minute," said the foreman on the other end of the line.

"Wait a...? How dare you! Tell me what's wrong. It sounds like murder down there."

"It's... one sec."

"What is it?"

Despite his protests, Ronald found himself faced with relative silence, until the foreman returned to the phone.

"Um, we've found something else."

"Oh God, what is it this time?"

The foreman paused for a moment, trying to find the right words.

Unfortunately, they never came, so he just said what he saw.

"It looks like a body."

3

Unlike good news, bad news has a peculiar habit of spreading as far and as wide as possible in a short space of time. While a celebration may be muttered once and left to fade into the ether, a disaster will become information-crack. It will jump from person to person with the viral capability of a sneeze, before expanding to such a degree that the minority will be those who *don't* know of it.

Hence before Laura could return from the bar, it had already been established that the fatberg was, in fact, full of corpses.

Even if it wasn't.

The origins of this fact-parasite had begun after the West Crumb Fatberg had seen two feet of detritus removed, exposing an inner layer that was fleshy in nature. Upon first sight, the crew working on removing the mass thought it nothing more than rubber, until more was exposed and the similarity to skin was too much to dismiss. Once this was reported, the more curious minded of the workers decided to stab at the flesh, producing a small bleed to occur.

At that moment, it was decided to leave well alone.

The whispers gathered below, and soon filtered out via text, direct message, and various social media. By the time Joey had seen it on his news app, it was becoming moderate news.

Theories wandered from the macabre – the aforementioned

balloon of bodies – to the absurd – a giant tumour fed by toxic waste. Of course, at this early moment, it did not matter what it was, except that it had been found, and people were talking.

Laura couldn't quite believe it, but the slight haze of inebriation helped make it more palatable. While there was still no visual evidence toward the nature of the now-named Fleshberg, imaginations ran wild enough to give it life. Joey flicked through the various representations for Laura, who zoned out out once artists started applying eyes and tentacles.

"That's ridiculous," she said.

"It's happening," Joey said.

"Says who?"

With a shrug, Joey gave the stock answer for his generation.

"Internet."

"You know better than that," Laura said, taking her seat and embracing her drink once more.

"Maybe, but *they* don't," Joey said, motioning toward the various other patrons. Sure enough, the whispers had penetrated all corners of West Crumb, and no matter how crazy the idea of the Fleshberg was, it was believable enough for the more mentally malleable.

Laura knew that they were only a few hours away from

hysteria.

-

Ronald was also aware of this. Mostly because he was seeing it first hand.

His phone had taken a life of its own, alternating between ringing, flashing, and fielding various calls, counter calls, and conference calls. Aaron, previously hired to simply help Ronald wade through the questions of the media, had gone into full-blown damage control. Ronald was now only a small cog in a larger machine, and that machine was chugging away fast.

And all the while, the two members of The Bureau stood there, taking it all in.

Right now, Ronald was on the phone to Debra Engel, head of the local water services covering the whole of Crumb. The health and safety associated with tackling the fatberg had been drastically changed by its new status as the Fleshberg. Words such as "biohazard" were thrown about with abandon, along with "lawsuit" and "disease". The general consensus was to get the cleaning crew out straight away, and look into extracting whatever was connected to the exposed skin.

It was a familiar question that Ronald was presented with.

"What are you going to do?" Debra said.

"What can I do?" Ronald said. "I've got a big smelly mess down there that, suddenly, contains a person."
28

"So you're saying it is a person?"

"I don't know? Maybe? Possibly?"

"Because if my team are handling a dead body, that is seriously outside their remit."

"They've never fished out a corpse from a lake before?"

Ronald had never been good with humour. He was saved by another call, but soon realised his telephonic salvation was actually another step into the circles of his own private Hell. It was Kenneth Wade, the local MP for Crumb.

Naturally, he was not happy.

"I've had a call from the Prime Minister, Ronald."

"Really?"

"Yes. She isn't happy."

Ronald had no idea how she had found out.

"Well, I'm dealing with it, sir."

"Dealing with it? You don't sound like you're dealing with it. You sound like you're panicking."

This wasn't entirely incorrect. For some reason, even though he was a mere civil servant, Ronald had become head of the Fleshberg Committee. And because of that, he now had to answer to the Prime Minister.

"No panic here, sir. It's all under control."

"They're saying bodies, Ronald. Plural."

"We don't know that yet…"

"This is too much for a serial killer. They think there's a cell."

"A cell?"

"Terrorists, Ronald. Threats to the country."

"It's… it's just a big smelly mess, sir."

"It is indeed, Ronald. A very big, very smelly, mess."

When faced with true authority, Ronald always found it difficult to find his words. Luckily, before he could get lost in an eternal stammer, an unlikely ally stepped forward and removed the phone from his hand.

"Hello?"

"Hello? Who's this? Where's Ronald?"

"This is Treadwell, with The Bureau. We are monitoring accordingly."

Ronald watched in shock as the female suit now known as Treadwell engaged in a series of nods, affirmatives, and passive dismissals. After only 3 minutes, the call ended, and Ronald was rewarded with a smile.

"Carry on," Treadwell said.

He wanted to ask, but instead Ronald answered the phone as it burst into life again, and listened to the questions of the local press as they asked about the possibility of a giant baby being created within a womb of rubbish.

-

"A giant baby?"

The latest rumour had swiftly reached the World Wide Web, but was given as much digital life as all the other theories that had spawned. The Fleshberg was now both a monster, a tumour, medical waste, and misidentified as a simple hot air balloon.

What interested Laura, though, was the new team arriving into the town.

In between salacious stories, the government were now here to study the Fleshberg. Various vans and trucks had flooded West Crumb, and despite their attempts at anonymity, it was obvious they weren't the usual merchants who partook in the local market. Men and women dressed in important suits, with important expressions, stepped out and looked around the town, and eventually they were replaced by hazard-clad beings ready to dive into the depths of the Fleshberg.

And yet, all around her, Laura saw people gawp at computer-generated images, reading stories of the bizarre and insane that, nonetheless, were more interesting than wet wipes and cooking oil. The idea of something interesting in West Crumb had indeed reached fever pitch, and while the populace revelled in this, scientists and experts slowly made their way through the crowds.

It was all too much for Laura, who finished her pint, and bade Joey farewell. As she meandered through the numerous crowds gathering both in the pub and in the street, she gave the odd glance to these new strangers in her town.

Their faces were, indeed, very serious.

And this made Laura very uncomfortable.

4

That night, the mere idea of sleep was a majestic notion that remained firmly out of reach for Ronald Pile. Both Treadwell and her partner Keating had happily dismissed him as the cacophonic avalanche of calls continued well past his contracted hours, and exclaimed how much they looked forward to seeing him tomorrow.

The whole thing for them seemed like one big lark.

In any case, as Ronald had walked home, past the ever-growing crowd of official looking people from no office Ronald had ever heard of, he couldn't help wondering what he had done to earn this mess. Not that the Universe was one for destiny and such, of course. But Ronald did consider how, if he had taken that job at Moira's brother's place, he'd be a spectator and not a participant to this chaos.

Once he got home, gave Moira a kiss, and patted their lurcher Bonnie on the head, he felt the pressure lift. One thing he had always been able to do was to leave the work at work and embrace home as a separate, wonderful world.

Then his phone went off. Saying Unknown Number.

As per his habit, Ronald didn't answer.

But Unknown Number was persistent.

Ready to give whoever it was a tongue lashing the likes of

which had never been heard before, Ronald was instead surprised to be greeted by a familiar voice.

"Hi, Ronald, just a quick thing," Treadwell said, sounding far too jolly.

"What? You said I could go home."

"Of course. But life never sleeps, does it? And neither do we, you know. Well, you don't know. But anyway, we need you to think over some stuff."

"Stuff? What stuff?"

"Criminal stuff."

Ronald did not want to think of criminal stuff.

He also didn't think it was his job to think of criminal stuff.

Alas, the duo from The Bureau had made it his job. They had pulled their strings and spoken to the right people in the right places, and made Ronald their number one guy. Naturally, he did not want to be the number one guy, or even numbers two, three, four or five. And yet, as Treadwell explained, they liked him.

"Keating alone has said what a wonderful impression you made on him."

"I... we didn't even talk. He just kept scowling at me."

"That means he likes you."

"What would he do if he didn't like me?"

Treadwell just laughed, and the call ended. Just as he had entered the safety of his home, his work life had invaded like a fly through the window. And much like that fly, it now had no idea how to leave.

This left the particular buzz of "criminal stuff" to irritate Ronald throughout the night. He didn't even enjoy his cocoa.

-

It was a different state of affairs for Laura, thankfully. The combination of several pints and a vegetarian kebab had made sure that when her head hit the pillow, she was out like a light.

Of course, only mere hours later, the very same combo was now assaulting her bowels like a boxer on amphetamines.

Unfortunately, much like all of West Crumb, she still had the horror of an overflowing toilet, so it was no longer a case of simply sitting down and letting nature take its course. Instead, nature now visited a bucket that was swiftly covered with a wooden chopping board to hide any foul smells that emanated from the remains of Laura's night out. By the time dawn rose and the birds outside called out for some feathered booty, the bucket was now at critical mass, much like the toilet.

With no other options, Laura tried sneaking out and throwing it down the drain.

36

Of course, much like all unique plots, everyone else had the same idea, and Allard Avenue now resembled something out of the bad old days, when a sewage system was a literal pipe dream.

She did her best to try and ignore this banal nightmare, and instead focussed on curing her hangover, getting various papers together for her course, and mindlessly scrolling social media. Naturally, the Fleshberg of West Crumb was big news now, with the more macabre details being front and centre. The headlines were as amusing as they were varied.

KILLER'S BALL OF GORE

GIANT BABY – WHEN WILL IT BE BORN?

SECRET SOCIETY OF UNDERGROUND BALLOONISTS

As always, they were all hyperbolic nonsense, but then through the mist of insanity came her reasonably sane voice.

Unfortunately, he had brought with him one of the least sane ones.

The problem was that Joey, having interests that welcomed the more curious elements of mankind, had friends that were so outside of the box that they doubted the existence of the box. They would debate you until you couldn't give a shit about boxes anymore.

This friend was Kevin, and he was giddy about the Fleshberg.

After a series of messages and bribes of lunch, Laura agreed to meet up with Joey and Kevin, mostly because the smell of Allard Avenue was getting worse.

And mostly because, sometimes, Kevin's theories could be fun to listen to.

-

Upon arriving at his office, Ronald finished his third cup of coffee and brewed up a fresh batch to get him through the next hour or two. The bags under his eyes were more like shipping containers, and his overall look made dishevelled seem stylish.

More annoyingly, Aaron and the duo from The Bureau were as chipper as usual.

Well, Treadwell and Keating were.

Well, Treadwell was.

"Bad news, Ronald," Aaron said.

"Of course it is. What else is there?"

"They're saying the Fleshberg is a symbol of society's ills."

There were too many syllables in that sentence for Ronald to completely comprehend, but he got the gist.

It was bonkers.

"They're saying the Fleshberg caused everything to be bad?"

"It's the media, Ronald. Of course they are. The Fleshberg is now England's scapegoat, and you're the face of it."

Ronald didn't like being the face of anything, let alone a Fleshberg.

"There's more bad news."

Ronald sunk into his chair and stared into space.

"It's bleeding, Ronald."

"It's *what*?"

"Bleeding. As in producing blood."

"I know what bloody bleeding is, you twonk," Ronald said, recalling that a previous prod by his former cleaning crew had produced some plasma. "How bad is it bleeding?"

"Rivers."

"Sewer rivers?"

"For now. But who knows? And this blood could contain diseases, Ronald. AIDS. In the water, Ronald. The water our children drink."

It was becoming all too much for Ronald. Thankfully, before he could fully commit to a nervous breakdown, The Bureau once more came to his aid. So to speak.

"Aaron?" Keating said.

"Yes?"

"Fuck off."

Aaron couldn't believe what he heard, but he was also aware he could not say anything back. Not after everything he had been told behind closed doors.

So naturally, off he fucked.

This left Ronald in the ominous company of Treadwell and Keating, the two casual suits from the mysterious Bureau. Before, they had just stood there and watched the whole thing, respectively smiling and scowling. But now, events needed a more proactive approach.

"Ronald," Treadwell said, "how ambitious are you?"

"Not very."

"Doesn't matter," Keating said, locking the door.

Suddenly, Ronald felt very nervous about what he was becoming part of.

But once a substantial pay rise was mentioned, he suddenly felt great.

He was no longer helping Crumb County Council, or the Prime Minister of the United Kingdom.

He was helping The Bureau.

5

Kevin was exactly what you'd expect from someone who watched a lot of conspiracy videos online.

As Laura arrived, she barely had time to sit down before his enthusiasm dominated the table. Luckily, she had already texted Joey her culinary demands for such a meet-up, and a fine mix of mozzarella sticks and wings were en route.

Not to mention the hair of the dog. Literally. The pint was called Hairy Dog. It was a popular beverage amongst her fellow students.

Straight away, Kevin had listed numerous theories, sub-theories, and counter-theories to the sub-theories. He had a manic energy that Laura didn't know whether was due to paranoia or too much caffeine, but she saw why Joey hung around with him. Yes, his exuberance for all that was questionable was exhausting, but it was a Hell of a show.

"So what do you know about the Fleshberg?" he finally offered to the rest of the table.

"It's a big mound of flesh," Joey said.

"Well... yeah... but what flesh? Whose flesh? If it is a who?"

"Who?" Laura said. It was a question mixed in equal parts

hangover, confusion, and triggering Kevin.

The latter worked.

"Exactly. Who? Are we talking medical experiments that have been flushed away like a discarded foetus?"

"Dude…"

"Hey, the truth is ugly, my friends. It's graphic and disgusting and…"

Almost on cue, the food arrived.

Taking a moment to enjoy a heady combination of cheese and wheat-based wings, Joey took over the conversation by noting the on-going presence of some sort of officials in West Crumb. These were the figures that unnerved Laura as much, and she was eager to ask more questions.

But before she could, Kevin had the answers.

"Secret government cabal."

"What does that even mean?" Laura said.

"What do you think it means?"

"A load of bollocks, if I'm honest."

Kevin laughed. "That's what they want you to think."

"That they're a load of bollocks?"

"Maybe they're made of bollocks," Joey said, mid stick. "All serving the Mega-Bollock below."

While most normal people would take this as a bizarre joke, Laura could see Kevin wasn't normal.

"You might have something there," he said.

"Really?"

"Why not? You don't know what the Fleshberg is. It could have grown from deep underground, a malevolent force of nature getting its vengeance against a proud and sinful populace. And those mysterious figures? Have you ever seen their faces?"

Laura hadn't. They were either decked in hazmat suits, riot gear, or general military fatigues.

But she had to remind herself that Kevin was a loon. They weren't mutants from below the Earth.

She was pretty sure of that.

Pretty sure.

Maybe she just needed more Hairy Dog.

-

Talking of too much pride, Ronald was brimming with the stuff at this point.

For so many years he had felt like a minor cog in the machine of government, but now he had been plucked from that tiny automaton and placed in the juggernaut of The Bureau. Treadwell and Keating had talked him up a storm, polishing his ego and promising all sorts of responsibilities and opportunities for leading the charge of the Fleshberg.

Not to mention the new pay cheque he'd be receiving.

He was so chipper, in fact, that when Aaron returned from whence he'd fucked, he just sat there with the biggest smug grin one could in these circumstances.

"You seem happy for someone who's on top of a big pile of shit," Aaron said.

Ronald smiled and shook his head in a cocksure manner.

"It's a Fleshberg, actually. Isn't that what you've got the media calling it?"

Aaron had taken note of this new confidence. He didn't like it.

"Ronald…"

"*Mr* Pile, please."

"Excuse me?"

"You address me as Mr Pile, not Ronald."

"Now you listen here you little…"

"Careful, Aaron," Ronald said, getting up out of his chair with puffed chest and jutted chin. "You wouldn't want to say something out of turn."

"Out of… do you know who I am?"

"I do. But you don't seem to know who *I* am."

Aaron laughed. "Oh I know who you are. You're a little man in a little office trying to be a big dick when you're barely an acorn. Not only that, but you're seen as a fool who can't answer a simple question, let alone solve a problem like the Fleshberg."

Ronald took a breath, slowly came round to the desk, and squared up to Aaron.

Unfortunately, the media advisor was a good 6 inches taller than Ronald, so it lost some of the effect.

Still, he kept his confident momentum going.

"You're wrong, you little shit. Don't worry though, I'll correct you. My name is Ronald Pile. And, yes, I'm in charge of sorting out this Fleshberg. But the only reason I'm seen badly by them out there is because *you* are bad at your job. You're supposed to be spinning this, when you couldn't even turn a phrase."

Ronald was particularly proud of that last comment.

"Look, even the best artists can only produce shit when given shit…"

"But the greatest can make shit look like gold, even if it's still shit. And they told me you were great…"

"I am great. I'm the best the government has. Whereas you…"

Ronald laughed, putting more effort into it than necessary. It made him seem like a parody of a movie villain.

"Oh, Aaron, I'm no longer part of your *government*."

"You what?"

Ronald puffed himself up even more.

"I'm… with The Bureau."

A sudden silence sucked into the room as all the tension, all the ferocity, imploded like a tiny star. Both men just looked at each other - Ronald with his proud smile, and Aaron with utter disbelief and more facial contortions than an abstract painting.

Before it eventually collapsed into intense laughter.

Ronald's smirk shifted slightly.

"You? The Bureau?" Aaron said, before laughing even harder. "You don't even know who they are!"

"I… I know I'm part of them."

Aaron shook his head. "Even so…"

More laughter, this time loud enough to make everyone in the surrounding offices wonder what the punchline was.

After falling into a chair and taking a moment to collect himself, Aaron Stone looked outside the window, shook his head, and then looked back at Ronald.

"OK, *Mr* Pile. You want me to spin this for you?"

"Er, yes. Yes!"

Aaron nodded and stood up again. Ronald waited for him to say something else, but nothing came up - other than another chuckle about him being in The Bureau.

He wasn't sure why this was so funny, but Ronald was sure that he was now important. And that meant he had to do important things.

Like sorting out the damned Fleshberg.

-

Meanwhile, too much proverbial dog hair had left Laura back in an inebriated haze that she did not care for this early in the day. Therefore, she vowed to meet up with Joey later, and maybe also Kevin as well - although she preferred to leave the latter with his online conspirators.

The wander back to the flat was short, but not without incident. In fact, there probably wasn't any incident, it was just the idea of now being surrounded by either secret government agents or mutant beings from below the Earth added to her anxiety. Every figure that stood in uniform, or emerged from the sewers below, was greeted by a firm glare by Laura.

Whether she knew she was doing it or not.

It didn't matter. She was nearly home, where she could fall into an afternoon nap and hopefully emerge a little better off. Unfortunately, upon entering Allard Avenue, she was greeted by a fleet of official-looking vehicles.

Unloading portaloos.

Naturally, a sober mind would see this as simply offering a temporary fix to the absence of usable amenities in people's households. But when bumping into a masked officer, Laura lost all sense of rationality.

"Monsters!"

"Eh?" the masked office said.

There wasn't much more to say though, as Laura rushed to her home, entered her flat, and collapsed on her bed.

With the knowledge that her little outburst would cause much cringing soon enough.

6

Feeling quite pleased with himself after the confrontation with Aaron, Ronald was now treating himself to a cookie from the mobile lunch van. Yes, it was vastly overpriced and inferior to most other cookies one could get from the supermarket, but he was part of The Bureau now, and could afford such luxuries.

Talking of his new employers, Treadwell and Keating returned from wherever they had gone to – Ronald in fact not noticing they had left in the first place – holding something in a large backpack.

It was placed with a glassy thud on his desk, and a mild pause wafted around the office as Ronald was mid cookie bite.

"Yes?" he said, with a mouth full of chocolate chips.

"The latest from the Fleshberg," Treadwell said, as Keating unzipped the pack.

While Ronald wasn't aware he'd made any decision recently about what to do with the Fleshberg, he just assumed he had done and now the Bureau's representatives were reporting back to him. Or did he report to them?

To be fair, the whole arrangement wasn't very clear.

What was clear, soon enough, was what the backpack contained. Keating lifted out a large glass container, which included contents that made Ronald regret the cookie.

"What the Hell is that?"

"What do you think it is?" Keating said.

"A lump of meat?"

"Well that's what it is."

It was, in fact, a biopsy from the Fleshberg, cut away by the team that now worked on investigating the large, biological mass. A small layer of epidermis sat listlessly on top, while the rest of the chunk consisted of a variety of muscle, sinew, fat, and unidentified viscera. While it wasn't as bloody as Ronald expected, there was still a fine pool of dark red plasma congealing at the bottom of the jar.

"And... so..." Ronald said.

"Don't worry, it didn't harm the Fleshberg," Treadwell said.

"Oh. Good?"

"Not really," Keating said. "We managed to confirm that it has regenerative properties. You see, we had one of our Field Agents burrow into the Fleshberg, for research purposes. Long story short, he was about 10 feet inside the Fleshberg when the severed opening behind him closed at a rapid rate."

Ronald could feel his jaw hanging, leaving him looking rather gormless.

"What happened to the Field Agent?"

"What do you think happened?"

Now Ronald was really regretting the cookie.

"Tests are continuing," Treadwell said, "so in the meantime, we just need you… to carry on doing what you're doing."

"Which is?"

"Exactly."

Looking at the fresh flesh now adorning his desk, Ronald grimaced and wondered if he would ever eat steak again.

-

It had been a while since Laura had eaten steak, and to be fair she didn't miss it.

A bacon sandwich, however, was a different matter.

The best she had when it came to the post-drink nap snack was a brand known as Fakon and, while it was alright, it wasn't the real thing. Hence why she put more salt on it than humanly necessary.

Out the window, she saw the new rows of portaloos being used by the residents of Allard Avenue, all while being guarded by the same masked officers she had mistaken for… something… when under the influence.

As predicted, the memory made her cringe.

The whole thing was starting to enter a state of controlled panic that didn't sit right with Laura. She was never one for the protest movement, along with Joey, and so the idea of being at the epicentre of a potential government takeover seemed like the start of more effort than she wanted to expel.

Therefore, she devised the new plan of going to see her brother down south. He was always good for a visit, and had excellent access to above average takeaways and palatable drinking establishments. So without further thought, she threw some clothes into a bag, swung it over her shoulder, and left the flat.

She got as far as the train station before reality hit.

See, one thing she forgot about a modern totalitarian movement was that they weren't much for letting people wander about willy-nilly. Sure, the residents of West Crumb weren't restricted in their daily routine, but if it meant going outside the town? Well...

"What do you mean, I can't leave?"

"Um, you can't *leave*?"

The masked officer at the station had stopped Laura as soon as she approached the ticket booth. Like other would-be travellers, she was swiftly informed that no trains were going in or out of West Crumb. Laura soon found that this also applied to cars, taxis, buses, and any other sort of transport vehicle that had the ability to breach the border set by the officials.

Pissed off was an understatement.

"What if it's an emergency?" Laura said.

"Is it an emergency?" the masked officer said.

"Sure. Why not?"

"Oh. Um... one moment."

The officer turned to one of his fellow goons and mumbled out of Laura's earshot. The other officer looked at him, shrugged, and then mumbled to another officer.

This went on for about four or five officers.

Eventually, a more official looking official came over, and greeted Laura.

"You have an emergency?" she said.

"Yeah, which means I have to leave," Laura said.

"I'm sorry to hear that."

The two stood there for a moment.

"So can I go?"

"No."

"Why not?"

The Official Officer paused for a moment, before telling Laura to wait there.

Instead, she texted Joey for a coffee and left.

Truly, the revolution would be trounced by incompetence.

-

Competence wasn't a problem for Ronald, though. No siree. Everything was under control - he had Aaron doing a far better job of representing him in the media, and he was part of The Bureau.

Even if that meant having to look at a gross pile of gore in a jar.

Still, Ronald knew that things couldn't get any worse.

Which means, of course, that they would immediately get worse.

In this case, it was courtesy of one word from Treadwell.

"Tendrils?"

7

While Laura's dwelling wasn't exactly palatial, it was a mansion compared to Joey's dwellings. He lived in a studio flat in the very basic sense of the word, consisting of one room with an en-suite bathroom. Not that he minded, of course; he described it as his own personal social cell, away from the masses and neatly packaged all in one place.

The smaller living area meant that he had more money to spend on luxuries, such as a coffee maker that seemed to produce liquid glory.

"So we're living in a police state," he said.

"Yep. Full blown Big Brother," Laura said. "If Big Brother had the competency of the worst slapstick comedians."

This didn't surprise Joey. Then again, very little did. It's why he was a good person to know - able to digest information, no matter how out there, and process it accordingly.

"Well the university is closed, but the pubs are still open. What could go wrong?" he said, calmly sipping his coffee.

"The fact that we still have a massive tumour under the High Street?"

"And beyond."

"Beyond?"

"Yeah. Apparently it's longer than they thought. Or it's grown. Couldn't really understand what Kevin was saying..."

Laura rolled her eyes at the mention of Joey's conspiracy theorist friend.

"By the way, he likes you."

"What do you mean?" Laura said, before it dawned on her. "Oh God... why?"

Joey shrugged. "You're female, attractive, and showed an interest in his ramblings."

"I was being sarcastic."

"Yeah, he's not good with sarcasm."

"Well this just gets more fun, doesn't it? What next? The Fleshberg explodes and turns us all into extras from Dr Moreau?"

"Dunno. But Kevin wants to meet up again. I mean, mainly with you, but I wouldn't worry about that."

Downing the rest of her coffee, Laura shook her head. "No. No more alcohol. I've already drank far more than the average person should, let alone the average student."

"Have you met the average student?"

"Enough. If Kevin is going to clamp onto *us* and entertain *us* with his nonsense, it's not going to be at a bar or a pub. Maybe... I don't know. The park?"

Of course, they both knew this would never happen. Besides, the local park was full of masked officials now, who were suspiciously poking into the soil with big sticks.

-

The footage being played in front of Ronald was equal parts confusing, terrifying, and badly lit. Supposedly, as Treadwell and Keating told him, it showed a member of their underground team looking over the Fleshberg, and noticing small lumps around the surface. At times, these lumps seemed to wriggle, before one popped open and revealed what looked like a finger.

Innocently, Ronald thought it was the officer who was absorbed by the Fleshberg, but The Bureau agents reliably informed him that they were very much dead.

Besides, the probing digit, while very fleshy, had far too many joints to be a finger. In fact, it twitched rather smoothly, bending at all sorts of angles in order to gain some idea of the world around it. One could almost call it sweet, like a newborn encountering the world for the first time.

But then, most would have the same reaction as Ronald, who as he squinted at the footage, saw more of the nodes pop open and reveal their own creeping sprout.

"I don't understand," he said, once the footage finished.

"I'm not surprised," Keating said. "You're not paid to understand."

60

"About that…"

"What it does show," Treadwell said, "is that the Fleshberg is showing signs of life. As you can imagine, this is very exciting."

"Is it?"

"Yes."

"OK. So what do I do now?"

"Handle it," Keating said.

"Handle it?"

"Yeah," Treadwell said. "Just keep on top of it."

"What does that mean?"

What it meant was soon made clear when Aaron entered the room, shuddered at the sight of The Bureau agents, and turned to Ronald.

"Why am I hearing about tentacles?"

"Tentacles?"

"Yes, Ronald. Tentacles. Slimy things that tend to grab people and pull them to their doom."

With that, Treadwell and Keating suddenly vanished from the office, leaving Ronald alone to explain the unexplainable.

"For one, it's Mr…"

"Don't Mr Pile me, not now. We've got a shitstorm ahead of us, and nobody has a bloody umbrella."

"I hardly think…"

"People are panicking, Ronald."

"Already?"

"This is a fast moving world. That footage is already on the socials."

It was true. The blurry video of the popping tendrils had already leaked, and was being shared at a rate of posts that not even the most naked celebrity could rival in virality.

Suffice to say, it was becoming one Hell of a day.

"So what are we doing?" Aaron said.

For a moment, Ronald wondered what they should be doing, and wished he could turn to his fellow Bureau colleagues for the definitive answer. Instead, he fell back on what he had learnt from local government employment.

"We deny it."

"Deny it?"

"Yes. It never happened."

"What never happened?"

"Whatever people are worrying about."

"What are people worrying about? What am I looking at? I mean, tentacles?"

"Nope."

"Nope?"

"A fancy video made by a bored mentalist."

Aaron could barely believe what he was hearing, not that he hadn't heard it from many low-level government wannabes before. But that usually revolved around sexy scandals, not mutant tentacles from below the Earth.

"So we're telling people there are no tentacles?"

"Tendrils."

"What?"

"Exactly."

The silence returned once more between the two, and Aaron decided to leave Ronald with his thoughts.

Said thoughts, of course, being wildly confused and bewildered, with a small hint of sitting on the edge of insanity.

And it wasn't even home time yet.

-

Sure enough, the leaked footage caused a stir once it got going. Over the course of half an hour, all the residents of West Crumb had seen the dark video of little spindly vines popping like horrific spots from the "skin" of the Fleshberg.

And while Aaron did his best to reassure excitable journalists – now from around the country – that all was well and the whole thing was a hoax, he knew there was one subsection that would soon throw all that out the window.

The mentalists.

Primarily, people like Kevin, who Laura and Joey found sitting with a big grin on his face in the middle of the pub.

8

If he was honest, Ronald was glad that it was the end of the day.

Ever since the Fleshberg had been discovered, he felt like his world had suddenly been turbo-charged. Sure, his mass consumption of coffee may have exacerbated that feeling, but caffeine alone couldn't cause the whirlwind of absurdity that he'd experienced.

As he made his way home, he considered all of the events that had unfolded. He had been hired by a secret government agency, to overlook the investigation of a giant mass of organic flesh that had been found under the humble high street of West Crumb. From there, he had then been battling with Aaron Stone about how the whole situation would be handled in the press, and the fact that a chunk of the Fleshberg now decorated his desk.

Oh, and one member of the Bureau's underground team was probably eaten by the Fleshberg.

And the Fleshberg was now sprouting.

It was all a bit much, now he put it all in perspective. Therefore, there was only one thing to do when he got back home to his wife.

Whisky, and lashings of it.

-

While he hadn't made the best first impression, Kevin was doing his best to make a worse second one on Laura. From the lecherous grin he gave her when she and Joey sat down with him, to his awful attempts to flirt therein, she knew it was going to be a long night.

She also knew the best way to deflect these clumsy attempts at romance would be to talk about the Fleshberg.

"Have you seen it?" he said, when the subject was brought up.

"Seen what?" Joey said.

"There's a video."

"Of the Fleshberg?" Laura said.

At the sound of this, Joey made the decision that more booze was required.

Laura wasn't keen on the idea of being left alone with Kevin. After a period that was spent in awkward silence and attempts at small talk by him that could be best described as woefully inept, Joey returned with a full tray of beverages and the subject of the Fleshberg footage was returned to.

It was the same footage that Ronald had seen, and that had duly been leaked by an unknown source. Of course, this didn't prevent Kevin from positing that it was an intentional leak by someone within the government themselves. Maybe even someone in their media team.

"That doesn't make sense," Laura said.

"Of course it doesn't," Kevin said, only slightly hurt by Laura's comment. "Why would it? Governments don't make sense. They don't need to. They just need to control."

"And this controls us how?"

"By spreading a climate of fear, duh. If we, the public, are made aware that this Fleshberg is alive and, apparently, eating people…"

"Eating people?" Joey said.

"Oh yeah, it's carnivorous. Apparently 14 of those mooks have been consumed already."

"Says who?" Laura said.

Flustered, Kevin just ignored her.

"The point is, we now know."

"Know what?"

"The truth."

"Which is?"

"That… that this Fleshberg is a monster!"

Theory-wise, it was weak. All Laura and Joey could do was sip at their pints.

"You don't believe me?"

"Dude, calling it a monster sounds… silly," Joey said.

"It's only silly because the semiotics of the word brings to mind fiction and nonsense. But is this nonsense?" Kevin said, showing the footage on his phone again.

Honestly, it was hard to say so. As Laura watched the small tendril poke out of its freshly burst spot and flick the air around it, she did feel the sense that what they were experiencing in West Crumb was something far beyond what they knew. This was straight out of science fiction, and that made all speculation no matter how weird valid.

Which was annoying, as this meant they'd have to hang out with Kevin more.

-

As Ronald finished his third whisky, he postulated with his wife, Moira, about what the Fleshberg actually was.

The first theory that came to mind was mutation, although even that seemed mad. But the way he described it, it made an absurd kind of sense; while he wasn't aware West Crumb had a large amount of radioactive waste stored deep within its sewers, he wouldn't put it past the previous regime to do something so heinous. After all, Gordon Jeffries – his predecessor – was hardly known as a man of fine character.

"So you think radioactive waste created this… thing?" Moira said.

"I can't think of anything else," Ronald said.

"Isn't it all… skin, and insides?"

The memory of his new gory desk ornament made Ronald wince.

"There does seem to be an organic element, yes."

"How does toxic waste do that?"

"Maybe… maybe through mutation of human material?"
"Like what?"

"I don't know. Toenails?"

"You think this has grown from toenails, Ronald?"

"It would explain the hard shell it was in…"

"The girls at the club think it's from semen."

Ronald nearly spat his whisky out.

"Semen?"

"Yes. Where men have been… entertaining themselves. Down the toilet."

"Are you quite mad, woman?"

"Ronald! Don't talk to me like that. Besides, it could work, especially with your toxic waste theory."

"OK, but… are you going along with the giant baby idea?"

Moira shrugged.

"Where was the egg?"

"Menstrual business?"

"Men…" Ronald put down his empty glass and considered another drink. Maybe straight from the bottle.

"Well you don't know what it is."

"That's what I'm trying to find out, my love."

"And how is that going? Or are you keeping with the toxic waste idea?"

There would need to be some admin to confirm Ronald's theory further, but right now he just wanted a single answer to the many questions that revolved around his head. In the end, his glass filled up again, and the idea of the Fleshberg being a giant baby was ceremoniously put to bed.

So to speak.

Until Moira's next theory.

"Could be an abortion."

This time, the contents of Ronald's mouth did project across the room and all over the carpet, and he had serious questions about what Moira got up to at her club.

As problems went though, that was minor. What Ronald had now was to look forward to whatever madness awaited him tomorrow. What disasters or horrors would unfold, and would more of them be placed on his desk?

However, there was one positive to be had that evening.

The toilet flushed successfully.

9

Humanity continues to work on the ultimate way to wake a person up in the morning, with the general idea being that the humble alarm clock is, by its very name, far too much of a shock to be pleasant. One consideration would be the smell of freshly brewed coffee, delightfully entering one's nostrils and triggering the senses into acquiring a brew as soon as possible.

Unfortunately, not everybody likes coffee. In this instance, however, Laura did.

What she didn't like was where she woke up – half-naked under the duvet, upon a mattress that rested on the floor, "Japanese style".

Or at least that was the excuse Joey gave.

Her startled eyes soon adjusted to the studio flat and caught the attention of its owner sitting on his chair, waiting for his drink to cool down.

"Morning," Joey said.

"Please don't say we…"

"Oh God no."

"Thank Christ," Laura said, sitting herself up and pulling the duvet to prevent any escape attempts by her breasts.

"You can do. He didn't brew you a coffee though."

Joey motioned to a second mug sitting beside the mattress, and Laura responded with a thankful smile and nod. It didn't answer all her questions though.

It turned out that after several drinks, Laura's state of inebriation reached a point where Joey made the decision to let her stay round his – it being the closest dwelling between the two – and sleep off the night's festivities in his bed. Meanwhile, he would flitter in and out of consciousness in his chair, until the dawn rose and it was an acceptable time for coffee.

"There's got to be more to it than that," Laura said.

"I mean, Kevin wanted to take you home."

The fear returned to Laura's eyes.

"Don't worry. You told him in no uncertain terms that would not happen."

"What were these terms?"

"I believe you said something along the lines of extracting his balls…"

This sounded about right.

"Oh, and the toilet is working again."

"Really?" Laura said, and in her eagerness to once more use an actual lavatory rather than the portaloos that had sprung up around West Crumb, she forgot about her semi-nudity and sprang into the en suite.

With a flush of the toilet, and sudden awareness of her undress, Laura grabbed a strewn T-shirt and asked the obvious question.

"How?"

Joey shrugged.

"OK... what did Kevin say?"

"He said the Fleshberg is absorbing the nutrients."

"Nutrients? As in..."

"People's shit."

Laura scowled in disgust.

"In fact, the whole evening was quite enlightening. After the video, and several more theories around the idea of mutant babies and secret government conspiracies, you really went on a questioning tear."

"How so?"

"Put it this way, you got Kevin far more excited than he would have been if you'd gone home with him."

"Don't make me throw up, Joseph."

"That'd be a waste of good coffee..." Joey said. "Anyway, you asked one question that made him go off."

"Which was?"

"Who does this benefit?"

It was an age-old question that Laura had always used against conspiracy theorists like Kevin, and sure enough it always lit a fire under their paranoid buttocks. In this case, it had meant that Kevin had now spent the night looking over all the facts, fictions, and fictions presented as facts, in order to share with them later.

This did not fit in with Laura's plans.

"You never have any plans," Joey said.

"Touché. Now, help me find my trousers…"

-

To his delight, Ronald's morning was far less adventurous. He was settling into the groove of importance that being with The Bureau had given him, and even treated himself to a chocolate bar to accompany the spring in his step. While the pressure of the Fleshberg still weighed heavily – especially after Moira's grotesque theories – a good rest had helped put all the mental files together and prepared him for the day ahead.

This was good, as the day ahead planned to be utterly ruthless with him.

Naturally, Aaron greeted him upon arrival. There was the usual grumbling of the leaked footage and what Ronald planned to do, but then what did *he* plan to do? There was nothing he could do now, so best just to get on with things behind the scenes.

"People don't want behind the scenes, *Mr* Pile," Aaron said. "They want answers."

"Well then, give them answers," Ronald said.

"Such as?"

"I don't know. You're the media guy."

"Quite. And as your *advisor*, I am advising you that something needs to be said to reassure the town. A press conference, perhaps."

The idea of hosting a press conference made Ronald feel very important, so he gave it the thumbs up and entered his office.

Where stood the second expected visitors, Treadwell and Keating of The Bureau.

"We've got news, Ronald," Treadwell said, chipper as ever.

"Yes, I know about the footage."

"Screw that," Keating said, less chipper as ever. "We've got the results of the DNA testing."

"Already?"

"We're very efficient."

"So it seems."

"Either way, here are the results."

Keating placed a large file on Ronald's desk. At first, Ronald looked at the binder confused, but then opened it to see a list of names that went on for nearly a thousand pages. A4 pages, to be precise. In a small font. Double-sided.

"What…"

"The Fleshberg contains the base DNA of nearly 800,000 missing people," Keating said.

"I don't understand."

"Well it's good news for those who are missing loved ones," Treadwell said. "But on the other hand, it does raise questions."

"Such as me not understanding."

"That's a given."

"But... if the... *Fleshberg*... is made out of missing people..." Ronald said, trying to find the words but just shaking his head in bemusement.

"We are doing further testing, of course," Treadwell said, "and also performing further dissections to study."

The mention of this drew Ronald's gaze toward his new desk ornament, in all its gory glory.

"In the meantime, we need you to carry on with what you're doing."

"There's the thing," Ronald said, getting up from his chair. "What am I doing?"

The confidence of the morning meant that finally, Ronald Pile was ready to confront The Bureau and get some idea of what his role actually was. If he was so important, he deserved to know why. After all, he now had a press conference to hold and wanted something good to present in it.

"You're a distraction," Keating said.

"A distraction?"

"Yes," Treadwell said. "You keep the public happy, give them someone to focus on while we do our work."

"I don't understand."

"You don't understand a lot of things. That's why you're the distraction."

"But... I thought..."

"You have good news for your little meeting, Ronald! You can tell them we've found all those missing people."

"In the Fleshberg?"

"In the Fleshberg."

"How is that good news?"

"Because, Ron, it's a riddle. A curiosity. Something so bizarre that it causes people to confuse themselves away from the potential reality of this situation."

Judging by Keating's tone – which was rarely ever positive – Ronald now felt very afraid of the answer to his next question.

"Which is?"

"Don't worry, you wouldn't understand," Treadwell said, her smile now seeming less friendly than it was before.

10

A lack of plan invariably involved a mooch around West Crumb for Laura, and while it was always amusing to snark around with Joey, an overnight stay meant that she'd prefer some time alone to gather her thoughts.

And many thoughts there were too. Not helped by the fact that, in the past, she could spend an afternoon wandering around town, eyeing stuff she couldn't afford in the shops, and grabbing some lunch as a precursor to a daily pub trip. Today, however, it felt more...

Constrictive.

The reason for this was the increased presence of the masked officials, who had since been given the wonderful nickname of Bergers, based on their arrival being the same time as the discovery of the Fleshberg. As she did her best to drift through the centre of town, she noted the different types of Bergers that were in West Crumb.

The first were the ones in hazmat suits, or the Toxic Bergers. These were the grunts that went underground, into the sewer, and got up close and personal with the Fleshberg. Laura knew this based on the video Kevin showed them the previous night. The most you ever saw of them were when they were coming in and out of the various manholes in West Crumb.

The second, and most prominent, were the Blue Bergers, although they dressed in black and not blue. The name, though, probably alluded to the fact that they looked like police, but were heavily masked with a sort of gasmask/bandana combo, and were possibly armed. Laura never actually saw them holding a gun, but they always seemed to have their hands fixed on something about their person.

The last set, and rarest of them all, were the Special Bergers. These had similar masks to the Blue Bergers, but dressed in black suits and always seemed to be on some sort of phone. It wasn't any phone Laura had ever seen marketed, and the suits also seemed a little… off. She couldn't quite put her finger on it, but it wasn't the kind of cut one could get at your local tailors.

In the end, the most disappointing fact about the Bergers was that none of them came with a side order of fries. Although that particular joke wasn't funny when Kevin had said it.

The competency of the Blue Bergers remained indifferent. Laura saw some locals try to get information, but they were met with the same mumbling incoherence that she had experienced at the train station. She overheard one elderly resident of West Crumb asking, rightfully so, whether they should wear masks as well.

"Probably," the Blue Berger said, and wandered off.

But while the Blue Bergers at least acknowledged you, the Special Bergers gave Laura a bad vibe. Yes, she felt suspicious of all of them since they first appeared, but at least the Toxic and Blue Bergers seemed to serve a purpose. The Special ones just seemed to be there, watching.

Waiting.

Feeling particularly daring, Laura strode up to one of them.

"What's going on," she said.

The Special barely flinched. They were on their device, listening and nodding along.

"Hey, I'm talking to you."

Still no response.

"Oi..."

Perhaps it was frustration coming to the boil, but the decision to grab the Special's arm wasn't Laura's best. Then again, while this was an unexpected action, the response was equally surprising.

The Special seemed to sigh, slowly turned to Laura and stared at her, saying nothing. Laura felt herself begin to sweat - although that could have been the hangover that was kicking in - and wondered why she wasn't letting go of the Special's arm.

Instead, she watched as the Special Berger nodded past her, and she was swiftly distracted by a Blue Berger.

"Everything OK?" the Blue said.

"Yeah, I..."

As Laura turned back, the Special Berger was gone. She couldn't even remember letting go of their arm.

"Um..."

"Excellent. Please move along. Or don't. Either way."

With that, the Blue Berger left, and Laura felt a cold shiver go down her spine.

-

There was something very motivating about a press conference, especially to those that craved a certain feeling of importance.

If he was honest with himself, this was a moment Ronald had dreamt of. Standing before the local press, holding court, and giving the kind of answers only an expert politician could give. Yes, this would be the moment he would announce himself not just to West Crumb, but the whole county.

Maybe even the whole country.

Little did he know how low his expectations were.

As he was gathering his notes, Aaron arrived.

"They're here," he said.

"Excellent. Conference room, I presume?"

"I thought about doing it in the smoking area, but you know."

Ronald laughed. "Don't get used to that sarcasm, Aaron. Remember, I'm…"

"With The Bureau, apparently."

"Exactly. So, who do we have? George from the Bugle? Daisy from the Newsletter?"

Aaron looked confused.

"My God, boy. Do you not know our local journos? The hard-hitters? The dogs of media war?"

As he said this, Ronald started to note the little smile on Aaron's face. He didn't like it.

"Oh trust me," Aaron said, "there's a lot of people out there I know."

And he wasn't kidding, as when Ronald stepped through the door he was greeted with the blinding wave of camera flashes going off. Cameras belonging to the world's media.

The room was packed to the brim with a veritable feast of ruthless journalists from all corners of the globe. Everyone, from the locals that Ronald had mentioned to obscure TV companies in furthest Asia, was here to hear his words on the Fleshberg.

He looked at his notes, and realised that it said very little.

"So," Ronald said, "who's first?"

What followed was a flurry of inquisition that Ronald Pile had only ever seen in movies. Questions came left and right, with Aaron playing conductor. Here came a volley from a major news channel in America. There goes a curious insight from the top paper in Australia.

Each question left Ronald as confused as the last.

"What is the Fleshberg?"

"Is it alive?"

"How many people are inside it?"

"Is there any truth to the theory of an underground terrorist cell of balloonists?"

The only answer Ronald could splutter out was full of ums, errs, and wells. He managed to get a few well-worn political answers out – "We're looking into it." "It's too early to say." "We don't suspect balloonists." – but eventually came the question that broke the camel's back.

"Do you think the people of West Crumb are to blame?"

"What? How?"

"Well, some say this is an ecological disaster. Given that the Fleshberg has formed in the centre of West Crumb, surely it is due to the populace here?"

"Now listen," Ronald said, feeling the fire in his belly return, "The fine people of West Crumb are simple folk. Good folk. Sure, they may flush the odd culinary remains down the drain, but who hasn't? And besides, this isn't a normal mass of waste; this is the flesh of nearly a million missing people. Explain that! Speaking as an official member of The Bureau, I can honestly let you all know that this is a very unusual, and very unnerving instance that we are taking very seriously."

The whole crowd of media went silent, before one member from the Far East put his hand up.

"Is… is this something very serious? As in, world ending?"

"Who can say? But let me tell you that The Bureau wouldn't get involved with any old big ball of condoms and cotton buds. This thing is weird, very weird, and we don't even know how weird yet. So maybe this is something that could end the world as we know it."

With this, the questions ended and various Dictaphones and cameras clicked off. The whole room looked very pale and confused, but Ronald felt great. He had stepped up to the world's media, and won.

What could go wrong?

-

Watching from a TV in the corner of the coffee shop, Laura was as dumbfounded as the rest of the clientele. In the distance, a mug shattered against the floor.

"We've got bloody Cthulhu under our streets," Laura said to herself, before thinking how she'd spend the potential end of the world.

She'd need something stronger than a coffee, that was for sure.

11

When performing a power play much like the one Ronald Pile just did, the main problem is the fallout that comes with it. For, you see, one cannot just unleash a grand gesture that will shake the status quo and expect for things to be relatively mild. In this instance, by insinuating that the Fleshberg was potentially a sign of the apocalypse, Ronald had lit the fuse on one hell of a social explosion.

What was worse was that he had name-checked The Bureau when doing so.

Upon returning to his office it was no great shock to see Treadwell and Keating waiting for him, firmly in their respective roles of good agent, bad agent.

The surprise came from the main area of their ire.

"Did you have to suggest an apocalypse?" Treadwell said.

"I don't think I did. I didn't even mention an apocalypse."

"You kind of insinuated one."

Ronald was pretty sure he hadn't. Then again he didn't know how the media worked, no matter how much he insisted otherwise.

"I thought you'd be cross I'd mentioned, you know, The Bureau?"

"Oh every crank and nutter mentions us," Keating said. "We've got protocols in place to sweep that."

In fact, the protocols went into place immediately after Ronald had name-dropped them. By the time the journalists had left the council building, any mention of The Bureau now referred simply to Crumb County Council.

The main issue was the fact that the Fleshberg would now be seen as a herald of the End Times. This meant that The Bureau would now have to work a higher level than they had been, and that things would start to get serious.

"How serious?" Ronald said.

"Very," Keating said.

"Oh. But wait a minute… I just did what you told me to do. Distract. Divert. I mean it's only a giant tumour."

The room fell silent.

"Isn't it?"

Treadwell moved forward and patted Ronald on the shoulder. Maybe it was supposed to be reassuring, but the force and overall unspoken tone of it suggested to him that he was now seen less as an asset within local government, and more part of the overall suppression in West Crumb.

Ronald Pile was more than likely out of The Bureau.

-

No sooner had the end of the world been inadvertently prophesised, panic set in around the small town.

While general looting and pillaging hadn't yet occurred, Laura still noted that the residents of West Crumb moved with a little more haste, and a little more animosity toward the Bergers.

The Blue brigade were doing their best to calm people and make sure a general message of everything being OK was passed out, but beyond them Laura could see the reality; the Toxic Bergers seemed to pick up the slack in their work, bringing in equipment that went beyond industrial and was almost otherworldly, while the Special Bergers were growing in number.

Laura didn't like this last detail one bit.

Still, it wasn't peak hysteria yet. Toilet rolls were still in abundance, and nobody was donning their sandwich boards and announcing things being nigh. Nevertheless, as Laura walked along the High Street, she felt more off than she had before.

For now the Fleshberg wasn't some curiosity, it represented something. Maybe a danger, maybe an oddity, but it was definitely something that she felt uneasy about. And for that, there was only one solution.

Luckily, Joey was one step ahead.

"So we're all going to die?" he said, pushing the ready pint into Laura's hands.

"Makes me feel less terrible about drinking for a third day in a row."

"I swear we did a week-long bender once…"

"I don't even know if we'll have a week to break that record."

"Better start drinking then."

The first pint disappeared as quickly as you'd expect from two students barely hiding their fear, and the second lasted only slightly longer. By the time the third was on their table, the pub was filled to the brim with other patrons looking to drown their terror, and the overall feel was one of foreboding.

A feeling Laura shared, but for other reasons.

"We're going to have to see Kevin, aren't we?" she said.

"Are we?"

"Come on, Joe. If anyone is going to know about this…"

"Yeah, point," Joey said, taking far more than the sip he intended. "I have been getting messages from him."

"And?"

"He's going mental."

"More so?"

"Again, point. But no, he's going on more about this Bureau. How they look into God-like creatures and general horrors come to life, and then cover it all up so we're none the wiser."

"So it's definitely a mutant then?"

"Are you being sarcastic?"

Laura sighed. "I don't even know anymore."

"Well, if we're all going to die, I'd appreciate a timeline. Yeah, they've closed the uni, but I still need to know whether I've got to spend my final days cultivating an essay on the French New Wave."

"I wouldn't bother. Just get pissed instead."

"Obviously."

And with that, the two toasted to their new plan of complete inebriation. After all, it was one way to spend their final days.

If, indeed, it *was* their final days.

-

As the world came to terms with the horror that rested under West Crumb, Ronald spent the rest of the day dealing with one societal headache after another. The problem with situations like this, he quickly discovered, was that while you could act swiftly and efficiently, it would be for nothing as, invariably, the lay of the land would shift more times than a skateboard during an earthquake. Every time he thought he had drafted the perfect response, he was suddenly told that the Prime Minister of Japan was declaring a ban on trade to the UK and it was his fault. Unexpected scenario followed unexpected scenario, and after a while he thought it best just to see where the cards fell and deal with it later.

Grabbing his coat, he saw Aaron on his way out and wondered if the young consultant was enjoying this.

It seemed he was not.

"You know, you could have helped me more," Ronald said.

Aaron was too distracted, though, with new footage that was playing before him. The Bureau's team underground had sent more film showing the Fleshberg, and the fact the tendrils were growing at an obscene rate.

And while Ronald found himself staggered by this, he also noted something else that was off.

"How did you get this?"

"I stole it," Aaron said.

"You stole video from The Bureau?"

"Yeah."

"Did… did you leak that footage?"

"Yeah."

"Why?"

Aaron was still staring at the monitor, seemingly transfixed.

"I don't know," he said, his voice a disturbing monotone.

Backing away slowly, Ronald made his exit. As he walked home amongst the drunken rabbles celebrating their perceived last days, he thought of how all this was getting very absurd very fast.

Then he remembered that Moira had been with her group today and began dreading what theories may have arisen.

Maybe she'll have created a cult.

12

Considering that a pending apocalypse would bring about some form of new normal, the idea of the pubs staying open because "fuck it" was not the most obvious scenario one would predict.

And yet, that was what came to pass. Something Laura considered as she and Joey left The Belle's View pub while the sun began to rise over the horizon.

Since then, various foodstuffs had been acquired, nibbled, then placed aside as the knockout effects of mass alcohol consumption took hold. This was why, upon waking, Laura had half her face covered in trifle.

Luckily, she was at her flat, and it was Joey's turn to arise in a state of confusion. Details were fuzzy between their brief food shop and their waking up, but while Laura was nicely on her bed, Joey was arranged on the sofa in a position that could only be described as torturous.

Then, once all her senses began to wake, the hangover kicked in.

Laura felt like screaming. Luckily, she thought better of it.

Instead, she cleaned the trifle off her face and noted that, in addition to various sweets, cakes, and assorted snacks, they had also purchased two full carrier bags of additional booze.

With a fear over what her bank account now looked like, she grabbed a can of cheap lager and cracked it open with a fizz.

Communicating only in a common grunt, Joey reached out to acquire one of the beverages. It tasted vile, but it was better than spending the day in eternal torment. After all, the world was ending, and it would be a shame to waste the lead-up to it in hibernation.

Laura then remembered. *The world was ending.*

Apparently.

While Joey attempted to get in a more comfortable position, Laura grabbed her phone and consulted the socials for the best idea of what was going on. These days it was far easier to get your news from social media than actual media as - aside from the obvious wave of racists, transphobes, and general nutters - you actually got a more honest idea of what was going on.

And what was going on was madness.

Not just localised to West Crumb either, although the night before suggested they led the way in complete frivolity. Various world leaders had come together to condemn the Fleshberg, and give many conflicting ideas on how to solve it. Everything from negotiation, to a full nuclear assault was put on the table, with the latter worrying everyone as it came from the President of the United States.

The more ground level reaction interested Laura more. It was a delightful mix of people not believing it was happening, or believing it so much they'd gone full loco. The British seemed to adopt the good old stiff upper lip, with the Fleshberg being blamed on drugs, teenagers, homosexuals, and immigrants.

And also cats, for some reason.

Nursing her can of cheap lager like a lost child, Laura curled up on the floor near Joey and waited for the alcohol to soothe away her throbbing everything, scrolling through various timelines for information. There didn't seem to be a general consensus on the Fleshberg or West Crumb as a whole, just an overall sense that the world was probably ending and that everyone had an opinion on it.

The one that worried Laura the most was from the nutters.

-

Sure enough, Moira Pile had joined a cult.

Well, maybe not a cult, per se, but Ronald believed her new devotion to her Ladies Group was as close to a gathering of madness as could be construed. Arriving home the night before, Ronald found she was not in and had instead left him a note advising him of the fact that she and "the girls" were staying in one location – strangely undefined – to come up with some ideas of what to do.

Because, as Ronald was finding out, everyone had an idea of what to do.

Except him.

And he was the one who *had* to come up with the idea, and do it.

The offices of Crumb County Council in West Crumb were a hive of activity upon his arrival, just not with people he recognised. A lot of them were the people the locals called the Special Bergers, rushing around with their stern masks securely attached to their faces, clicking away at devices in their hands. They seemed to be setting up some sort of command centre, which consisted of long banks of technology that Ronald had never seen before. And he'd tried to buy a laptop recently, so was aware of all the latest gadgets.

What then transpired was an assault on two fronts. The first was from Aaron, who waved a front page showcasing an archive picture of Ronald Pile with hair, under the headline PILE OF RUBBISH.

"That's a bit rude," Ronald said.

"It's the best we could get," Aaron said. "You're lucky you've not been crucified."

Ronald laughed nervously. Surely they hadn't reached the point of crucifixion yet?

"The press conference was, I think we can agree, a terrible idea."

"Yes."

"So what do you think we – as in, you – should do now?"

Ronald thought for a moment. Or, at least, he would have done, if not for Aaron's insistence on answering for him.

"Shut up."

"Sorry?"

"Just... do whatever you need to do with your Bureau friends, but leave everything else to me."

Now before, Ronald would have raged at this overt display of power grabbing but, truth be told, the whole thing was overwhelming him. It had devolved into one of those "be careful what you wish for" situations. The power in question had become more than he could handle, and now he wished he was looking at bin collection schedules again rather than mutants from below the Earth.

Which led nicely to interacting with Treadwell and Keating.

Neither said hello, as neither saw Ronald enter his office. Instead, while Treadwell reviewed footage on a monitor that Ronald had already been privy to - thanks to Aaron – Keating snapped orders down a phone.

It appeared that the tendrils emanating from the Fleshberg were growing faster than the so-called Toxic Bergers could cut them. Not only that, due to the size of the Fleshberg, there were whole areas where the tendrils were growing without impediment, which did not bode well when one thought too much of it.

So Ronald tried not to.

Until Treadwell saw him.

"Ah, Ronald. Lovely to see you," she said.

"Um, thank you?"

"Do you want an update?"

"That would be nice."

"Excellent. Because I'll happily give you one, even though I don't have to. In fact, not even sure why you've come into work, but hey ho. Anyway, those pesky tendrils keep on growing, and we've lost about... how many agents, Keating?"

"Eighteen."

"Eighteen agents to the Fleshberg."

Ronald didn't understand, so Treadwell continued.

"Possibly absorbed, Ronald, or simply vanished. Much like the near million that make up the Fleshberg's DNA. We're not sure. We just know they're not answering our calls."

"Oh."

"Meanwhile, it appears everyone topside has gone a bit loopy. Real apocalyptic reaction scenario. This is where you come in."

This surprised Ronald, as he wasn't sure the Bureau would trust him with anything ever again.

"We want you to try and... temper things. Keep everybody in a state of calm. Because, for some reason, this Fleshberg is making everyone a little..."

"Fucked up," Keating said.

"Exactly."

"How do I do that?"

"I don't care," Treadwell said, her tone contrary to the smile on her face. "Organise a bake sale or something."

"My wife has joined some sort of WI cult…"

"Fantastic. Get them to bake cakes. Maybe throw a fayre or fete. Leave the impending horror to us."

"Impending horror? So…"

"Like you said, Ronald, if The Bureau is involved, it's serious stuff. And it's only going to get more serious."

With that, Treadwell went back to watching the footage, where a Toxic Berger was seen climbing on top of the Fleshberg and then disappearing behind the folds of its mass.

Meanwhile, Ronald sat at his desk and did what he always did in situations where he was told to do busy work.

He grabbed a pen and looked busy.

13

Now that the hangover had been quelled by more booze – albeit with orange juice chasers so they didn't feel like complete alcoholics – it was decided the best thing for Laura and Joey to do was to head to their establishment of choice and camp there for the day. Besides, it would be more tolerable to take in Kevin's latest ramblings on the Fleshberg when surrounded by folk they knew.

Joey told Laura about the plethora of messages Kevin had sent him, which bordered on the verge of psychopathic mania. He seemed keen to meet with them for reasons best left unconsidered, although Laura did wonder if it was to further his unrequited crush.

Then again, the end of the world was coming. Maybe she should throw a dog a bone.

No, Laura thought. She had far more dignity than that.

The journey from her flat to The Belle's View meant trekking across the growing mad masses in the centre of West Crumb. The High Street, once home to a wonderful array of shops, markets, and food vendors, now seemed to play host to protestors, mentalists, and a mix of the two. Naturally, the mysterious Bergers tried to apply some sort of calm to these little pockets of resistance, but if Laura knew anything as a student, it was that if you tell people not to do something, they want to do it more.

Other than that, people just wanted to get on with their lives, ignorant to the potential danger that was literally under their feet. They chatted over coffee, perused barely-stocked shop fronts, and walked their assorted dogs and children. It was an interesting sub-group that only a country like England could produce – when faced with the threat of potential devastation, they throw two fingers up and carry on regardless.

Apparently, it was "Blitz Spirit".

This was nice and all, but largely impractical in the face of the apocalypse.

After making their crossing through the centre, Laura clocked sight of a small group who had converged near the council offices. There, a lone figure tried to hold court, only to be met by angry exclamations, veiled threats, and the odd rolled-up bit of rubbish.

For a moment, Laura felt sorry for the man. Then she saw it was Ronald Pile, the media's main source of all the trouble, and she laughed at the balls on the guy. Imagine being public enemy number 1 and stepping outside.

He had to be more drunk than she was.

-

In truth, Ronald Pile wasn't drunk. He was bored.

No matter how many spreadsheets he pottered on, or how many notes and lists he doodled, being surrounded by people far busier and far more important than he was began to grind him down. Ronald

105

decided that his form of authority would be best served on the streets, with the people. After all, unlike the media, they'd surely take his words with maturity and trust.

This was one of the many reasons Ronald hadn't gone far in politics.

Nobody from The Bureau's team acknowledged his announcement of leaving, and Aaron seemed far more invested in crafting some sort of new media campaign than to pay him any mind. So it was that Ronald quietly left the council offices and stepped into the heart of West Crumb.

Almost immediately he was besieged by pensioners.

"What's going on?" one said.

"I'm glad you've asked that," Ronald said, feeling confident he was now with his people.

"I'm not. I'm shitting my pants."

Ronald confidence waned a bit.

"Is it true that this thing is psychic?" an old gentleman said. "Because would that explain the weird dreams I've been having?"

"Dreams? No, as far as I'm aware the Fleshberg isn't psychic."

"Then why do I want to hug it?"

"I don't know."

The questions continued and grew in ferocity. Each time someone threw forward a new – and incredibly bizarre – theory or idea, Ronald felt his brain pickle a little bit more.

"Listen, I know you're all scared…"

"Scared? I was just mildly concerned."

"OK, that's good."

"But you said we should be scared."

"What I actually said was…"

"We're all going to die!" someone at the back shouted, and parts of the crowd stumbled away in panic.

Those that remained did not look the sort who took the Fleshberg in good nature.

"We know," one young man said.

"Know what?"

"What's *really* going on."

"Really?"

"Yeah."

Everybody waited for the next response.

"Well?" Ronald said.

"What?"

"What do you think is going on?"

The young man looked around.

"Government?"

"What?"

"Like, government testing. That's why all those missing people were found in the blob."

"The bodies were found?" someone said.

"Why don't you give them back to their families?" a woman said to Ronald.

"There are no bodies," Ronald said.

"What about the person in the video?"

The person the crowd member was referring to was the one who Ronald saw swallowed up back in his office. Apparently that had now leaked as well, probably through Aaron, although Ronald had no idea why.

"Can we go down there?"

"Why would you want to go down there?" Ronald said.

Nobody could give an answer.

"You're stopping us from going down there and learning the truth, aren't you?"

"Don't be stupid. We're not letting you down there because it isn't safe."

"It's not safe?"

108

"We're going to die!"

Cue further hysteria.

Ronald struggled through the crowd, now realising that if he listened to any more of this toxic stupidity his brain would leak from his ears. Unfortunately the crowd followed, asking more questions and providing the occasional *boo*. The more he moved into the centre of the High Street, the larger the throng grew. Disgruntled residents who were verbally attacking the Bergers joined the growing mass, deciding to make Ronald the new source of their ire.

Eventually, as he waded through the growing rabble, Ronald turned to them and raised his hands to talk.

"Listen, there's no need to panic. We have everything under control and nobody needs to be scared, concerned, mildly irritated or otherwise."

Behind him, there was the slow sound of metal against metal.

"I'll even get this fine service worker to explain," Ronald said.

As he turned, expecting to see the glow of one of the Toxic Bergers, he instead saw something that made him grimace.

Poking out the manhole was a fleshy tendril.

14

Upon arrival at The Belle's View, there was no amount of surprise to find the doors open and the clientele already in full swing. This came as no surprise to Laura, as she knew the universal truth that if you have a good idea, invariably everyone else has the same one. Especially when it comes to arriving early.

That said there was no real battle for the bar. The owner of The Belle's View, simply known as Das Barlord, had placed an honour system on most of the drinks, with a bucket serving as the till and access to the drinks mostly unrestricted. This allowed Laura to grab her and Joey a couple of bottles from a fridge and locate a table for them to await Kevin's arrival.

While they did so, the noble art of people watching was conducted. Laura knew the folk of The Belle's View well – a collection of characters from the very fringes of normality, who treated the upcoming apocalypse as a merry jaunt toward the next life. Whether that was the common theologies, or something straight out of science or fantasy fiction, didn't matter. All that did matter was community, and they were a big one.

It was actually quite sweet. Except for when one of them known as Mac started singing and everyone covered their ears in jest.

After an hour or so, Kevin arrived with a small posse in tow. Not being regulars of The Belle's View, they were treated to some curious looks by the locals until Laura greeted them and they were no longer seen as outsiders.

Kevin's group consisted of himself and three others:

Clyde, a shaggy haired Welshman who seemed to be constantly stoned.

Raven, a standard Goth Girl complete with a tattoo on every available patch of skin, and hair coloured the deepest black.

And Greg, the eldest who, quite frankly, just seemed odd.

Pleasantries were quickly dismissed as Kevin produced his laptop and eagerly set it up, not wanting to wait any longer to share his views with the already amused Laura and Joey.

"I mean, it's all kicking off now," Kevin said.

"You mean there's more than a world-ending blob?" Laura said.

"Oh, it's not a blob. It's something so much more - a new form of life, born from the remains of others. And much like all life, this is just its early gestation period."

Kevin began to tell Laura and Joey how the Fleshberg was now growing in the form of vines sprouting from its flesh. These, he believed, were to feel out the land around it, and potentially source another avenue of growth. From there, new Fleshbergs would be created, soon producing something more familiar to humanity.

"Like clones?" Laura said.

"Not like clones. More like... a new type of humanoid."

While Kevin's crew listened with enthusiasm, Laura was starting to see Kevin for what he was – a lonely guy who latched onto whatever weirdness would make him seem either popular or, at the very least, interesting. Sure, he seemed smart – Laura trusted Joey's choice of friends, given she was one – but it was an intelligence that had become unhinged due to a lack of social refinement.

Even as, with Clyde's help, Kevin sketched out what this potential new species would look like, Laura couldn't help but feel sorry for him. He had taken this very weird situation and made it into his new – and perhaps only – passion.

Which begged the following question.

"You don't think it's dangerous?" Laura said.

The stifled mockery from Kevin's friends pissed her off. Luckily, Kevin was more tactful.

"Typical media fear mongering," he said. "The only threat that life-form has is if you don't respect it as you should."

"Respect?"

"Yes, respect. Upon discovery of any new species you should approach with acceptance, not terror. Why should we be scared of it?"

"It's eating people?" Joey said.

"It's not eating people, it's absorbing them," Raven said, almost indignant at the suggestion.

"Isn't that the same thing?" Laura said.

Kevin tried to defend the point, but Raven continued.

"It's a choice. They've given themselves to be part of the new evolution."

By now, Laura could see that Raven was quite mad.

Then Greg spoke.

"The mass needs fresh blood to grow, like any burgeoning life form," he said. "Like the lost before them, these people have become part of something bigger than you."

The venom in his tone didn't sit well with Laura; she was tempted to suggest to Joey that they leave Kevin's cabal to the locals of The Belle's View.

Before she could, Kevin began to talk.

"Would you like to see it for yourself?"

"What?"

"The Fleshberg, would you like to see it?"

Laura smiled. "What do you mean?"

Kevin turned to his friends, and with a far too smug look, announced his plan to Laura and Joey.

"We're going underground."

-

Given that The Belle's View was situated far from the centre of West Crumb, everyone there was blissfully unaware of the chaos that was slowly unfolding.

As Ronald Pile had noticed when confronting the locals, the tendrils were indeed appearing topside. Not only did they poke up from under the various manholes, but small clusters of the meaty veins wriggled their way out of the many drains in the streets.

Public reaction was as obvious as it was anarchic. People ran, attacked the tendrils, or simply wet themselves. Admittedly, the latter was in a small minority, but as Ronald was part of that he felt it was important to include.

Another factor that was slowly becoming clear was the dilution of the Bergers presence. Whereas the Toxic Bergers – the ones going underground to interact with the Fleshberg – weren't the most obvious of agents, they had all but vanished from West Crumb. The Blue Bergers – the average goons, as Ronald saw them – were still there but lighter in number. In fact, those that had remained seemed ready to leave at the drop of a hat.

As for the mysterious Special Bergers? Gone, except in Ronald's office where they congregated with Treadwell & Keating of The Bureau.

Ronald was at a loss as to what to do. Several people turned to him for answers, but he was as confused and disturbed as they were. Instead, he engaged in various plumes of ramble, before making his way back toward the Crumb County Council building.

But upon arrival, he was stopped.

"Where do you think you're going?" the Special Berger said.

"Where…? I work here!"

"Not anymore."

"What do you mean?"

"Go home, Mr Pile. Relax. Everything is under control."

Whenever the phrase "everything is under control" was said, Ronald knew that everything was very far from being so.

"Listen, speak to Treadwell and Keating. They know me. They hired me! I'm one of you."

The Special Berger looked at Ronald, and then produced a device from their pocket. After a few taps of the device, they looked back up and nodded.

"Come back tomorrow."

"Tomorrow?"

"That's what I said."

"Why tomorrow?"

"Do you always ask so many questions?"

Ronald huffed his chest and was ready to get really cross, when the Special carried on.

"I've got a question."

"Oh. Err, what?"

"What's that smell?"

The smell was the result of Ronald's 'accident' upon seeing the tendrils pop up; it was now pungent enough to shame him into turning around and cleaning himself up at home.

But tomorrow? Oh they'd get the full wrath of Ronald Pile tomorrow.

If there was one.

15

As was fast becoming tradition in the post-Fleshberg world of West Crumb, the drinking in The Belle's View didn't stop because the law said so. Once the clock struck midnight, instead of last orders being called, a well-practised sign was relayed between Das Barlord and one of the regulars and the front door was locked.

And thus, the lock-in began.

Laura was rather enjoying this new normal, although that was mostly due to the fact that Das Barlord was serving up free shots of schnapps. Drinking itself was known to be typical student behaviour, and Laura had embraced it with open arms upon arriving in West Crumb. It didn't hurt that she was friends with Joey who, when he drank, could really put them away.

The hours slipped away nearly as fast as the various alcoholic substances in glasses, and Laura wasn't even aware that Kevin and his group had left to enact their plan to see the Fleshberg for themselves. Now she thought of it, she couldn't help but feel that it was befitting of the insanity that had struck the town. Of course Kevin – a noted fanatic of things outside the box – would want to see this anomaly for himself. And while she had been tempted to join in, the arrival of another drink had easily swayed her decision.

She couldn't help but wonder how they were doing, though.

-

Once he was freshened up and in a fresh pair of slacks, Ronald began the new chore of making his own dinner. Moira Pile was with her Ladies Group, and had been ever since the Fleshberg arrived.

To be fair, he was glad of the peace.

So naturally, it had to swiftly be shattered.

It wasn't that Ronald was disappointed that Moira had returned, it was that it wasn't the Moira he had married. She looked, sounded, and seemed like her, but the way she acted was even more unusual than normal. His wife had always been quirky, but this was something else.

"Are you finished with the group?" Ronald said.

"Oh no, we've still plenty to do," Moira said. "I've just come back to collect some things."

Ronald just silently nodded in acceptance.

"Are you OK?" she said.

"Me? Oh yes. Dandy."

Despite being in the midst of mania, Moira could still tell her husband wasn't in the best of places.

"Are you sure?"

"Well actually…"

"Because if you're not, you should come with me. Well, not *with me*, per se, but I'm sure the other husbands can cheer you up. I hear they're playing poker."

120

"I don't like poker."

"Oh. I guess you should stay here then."

Before his wife could disappear upstairs to pack some things and leave their marital home forever, Ronald had to know exactly what the Ladies Group were up to.

The response he got was very off.

"This could be a boon for the town," Moira said. "We want to get on that as soon as possible."

"You're thinking of *tourism*?"

"Oh, Ronald. You've been in politics too long. Your new role as a media figure has obviously warped your brain."

"How do you mean?"

"Everybody is saying it's all doom and gloom with the Fleshberg, but is it? How do we know it's not just some… plant?"

"You think it's a plant?"

"It would explain those vines."

Ronald knew that if Moira had seen them, she would soon realise they were only like vines in that they were thin, bendy, and spreading.

The pulsating veininess of them was quite different to your average flora.

As his wife rushed up the stairs, Ronald called after her.

"Moira, aren't you scared?"

"Scared? Don't be silly. This is the most exciting thing to happen in years."

"Listen, darling. I've seen video of this thing. I don't think it's as benign as you think it is."

"I'm sure you're just overreacting."

"It's eating people!"

There was no response from upstairs. Ronald stood there waiting, until Moira appeared again, suitcases in hand, and looking as giddy as she did when she came in.

"If it is eating people, there must be a reason," she said.

"I don't understand..."

Moira looked at Ronald, touched his face with a delicate stroke, and kissed him on the lips.

"Ronald Pile, you never really did, did you?"

And with that, Ronald's wife left him.

Literally.

-

As they staggered back toward Laura's flat, full of song and alcohol, neither Laura nor Joey took much notice of their phones. In all honesty, if they had, they would not have managed to make much sense of it anyway, their vision being as coherent as the lyrics they were hollering.

It wouldn't be until their bodies, no longer under the thrall of booze, would snap them awake that they would find out exactly what Kevin and his group had been up to.

They had, in fact, managed to get in the sewers under West Crumb. There was no longer any sign of the so-called Toxic Bergers, and in fact there was no impediment to their little mission at all.

Kevin, ever the instigator, had taken the lead in their rather smelly journey, and after a few wrong turns they began to get closer to where the Fleshberg was.

Then things went very wrong, as Kevin tried to tell Laura and Joey over the phone. He'd get the chance to tell them the next day, if he could put it into words. In the meantime, he had escaped the sewers and swiftly made his way home.

Alone.

The others had gotten too close to the Fleshberg.

-

And so, as West Crumb slept off their protests, wonderment, inebriation and assorted debauchery, the Fleshberg continued to grow.

Not in mass, of course, but the spindly little veins that had sprouted in great numbers from itself now prodded through drains, manholes, and any other break in the surface they could find.

As the dawn rose on the little English town, the residents were about to find themselves far closer to the Fleshberg than they anticipated.

16

Upon awakening, Laura noted the barrage of messages and missed calls on her phone. She had no idea how Kevin had got her number, and strongly suspected either a drunken Joey or a devious theft from his phone. But while that was her first concern, her second revolved around the contents of the messages.

I'VE SEEN IT

IT'S GLORIOUS

GOD

This was weird enough, but had nothing on what Joey received.

The duo had gone their separate ways during the night, but as was becoming tradition in this strange new world, they were to meet up to carry on their apocalyptic bender. Before this could happen, however, there were more pressing matters to attend to.

Matters that weren't on Joey's phone.

No, these matters protruded from Laura's various outlets. Her taps, plugholes, and even her toilet were now infested with the fleshy tentacles that were sprouting from the Fleshberg. Not only had they snaked themselves through her various amenities, but they also weaved their way out of her living room window.

As she struggled to take this in, she was oblivious to the chorus of panic that was rippling down the street.

In a dream-like daze, Laura glided to the window and saw that the tendrils had pulled themselves through every available pipe in the centre of West Crumb. While Allard Avenue was close, it wasn't close enough to be excessively infested with the vines.

That, as Joey tried to tell her, would be found nearer to where the Fleshberg lay.

For now, Laura just looked as dozens of the things had pulled themselves through folks' sinks and faucets, escaped through the nearest window, and limply wriggled their way toward West Crumb High Street. She caught the eye of a few of her neighbours, but nobody could easily articulate what they were seeing nor how they felt about it.

While tempted to go back to bed and hope this was, indeed, one Hell of a bad dream, Laura instead acquired a beer from her fridge, and started as she meant to go on.

After all, it would be easier to accept all this when slightly tipsy.

-

Living a little further from the source of the tendrils, Ronald Pile didn't have the full joy of waking up with a tentacle tickling his toilet habits. He only learnt of the huge growth of the Fleshberg's thick fibres as he reached the outskirts of the town centre, where many of them weaved out of buildings and slithered down the road.

The sheer fact that they were now visibly moving made Ronald feel a little sick. As tiny little growths upon the Fleshberg, they could easily be dismissed as the kind of epidermal abnormalities one would see in blood blisters or skin tags. But now, slipping along like grotesque worms, the idea of their biological status was more alarming.

Naturally, some people saw his council badge and asked questions.

"What the Hell is this?" one man said.

"Sorry?"

"You better be. What happened to cutting them down?"

"I... we were."

"Doesn't seem to have worked, does it?"

"I've just seen the town centre," someone else said, although neither Ronald nor the angry man knew where from.

Then again, they weren't sure they wanted to, as the person saying this sounded very hollow in mood.

Ronald tried to ignore the confusion and abuse that walked alongside him, and instead kept an eye on the tendrils. They seemed to come from all directions, but moving toward one specific place. Some, which he soon realised came from further outside the town centre, were still trying to inch their way along, while others stretched around corners and side streets to an unknown goal.

Of course, a more intelligent person would know what that goal was. But Ronald, being a bit too blasted by the absurdity of the situation, didn't do the maths until he entered West Crumb High Street.

There, in the centre of the road, where a manhole cover once lived, was a small cluster of the veins wrapped together.

And all the others were easing themselves along to join in.

Mouth agape, all Ronald could do was stare at this strange mesh. Around where he stood, some people tried to cut the tendrils apart while others were just happy to prod and poke.

One thing that he did soon note, though, was that all of The Bureau's agents in the field were nowhere to be seen.

-

Cutting the vines proved to be a fool's errand, as Laura found out when she tried to use her toilet. The outer skin of the tendrils was tough, leading her to believe it was a coating of keratin or super-advanced scar tissue. After many attempts to hack at it with various sharp implements, Laura resigned herself to crouch around her new accompaniments, and get the Hell out the flat.

Many others were soon finding themselves equally as thwarted by the strength of the Fleshberg's tentacles. On her way to meet Joey, Laura saw bread knives fired up, axes swung, and even a strimmer utilised with a certain level of aggression. Each time, she noted how the veins would shrug off each hit of a blade, and carry on pulsing their way down the road.

What was also curious was those who weren't attempting to destroy the veins. In fact, some seemed amused, or in awe of the mass of fleshy wiring that populated West Crumb. The odd domestic broke out over those who wanted to slay the appendages, and their partners who saw it as akin to decapitating a child.

In terms of madness, it certainly was a new flavour.

Naturally, Joey was located outside a coffee shop, where he had helped himself to a hearty brew in a pint glass.

"Irish?" Laura said.

"Natural."

"You not drinking yet?"

"Are you kidding? I want to see this with sober eyes first."

"Rather you than me."

"Besides, have you seen the texts?" Joey said, referring to Kevin's correspondence.

"To be fair, I've seen a few folk since who might be in the same boat."

"The 'Fleshberg is God' boat?"

"It seems to be a popular vessel."

Joey pondered this and, instead of subjecting Laura to the barrage of messages Kevin had sent about his near fatal revelation, simply her passed the pint of coffee and helped himself to a biscuit.

For now, Laura decided it would be best to join in with this sober viewing. Or, at least, as sober as her morning beverages would allow.

Especially as the snarling stump of tentacles was growing.

132

17

The ever-presence of The Bureau was seen as overkill when one looked at their arrival. But now, with the Fleshberg's sprouts bursting from the sewers below and converging into what looked like a stump, Ronald Pile believed that they were needed more than ever.

So it was with great surprise that, upon entering the council offices, he found most of them had gone.

The hive of computers, devices, people and fever was now a mere smattering. The Bergers – the agents who were the most sighted among their corporate horde – were no more. Instead, Ronald saw only a few suits with stern faces, and his old friends Treadwell and Keating.

The first thing he said was the most obvious.

"Where is everyone?"

"Belgium," Keating said, his eyes fixed to the laptop in front of them.

"Belgium?"

"Yes, Belgium. Country in Europe. Does good beers."

"And chocolate," Treadwell said in her jolly way.

Ronald knew this, but didn't know how it related to the predicament unfolding in West Crumb High Street.

"Do you know…?"

"We know everything, Ronald," Treadwell said.

"So… the stump."

"Pillar," Keating said, still engrossed in what was on his laptops screen.

"Pillar?"

Yes, pillar. In the time it had taken Ronald to reach the council offices, the streams of crawling tentacles had, in their convergence, become thicker, tighter, and taller.

In terms of growth, the Fleshberg's shoots had gone beyond rapid and now were firmly planted in 'constant'.

"Well, what do we do now?"

"We wait."

"Wait? Wait for what?"

"Ronald, we have this under control. Why don't you…?"

"No. No! I want to be a part of this. You said…"

"If you want to be a part of this," Keating said, finally glaring at Ronald, "then go sort your boy out."

"Boy?"

Keating spun his laptop around, and Ronald saw on the screen a live feed of the pillar of tendrils. He also saw, surrounding it, a small group of people fending off any attackers of the pillar.

Amongst them, as well as his wife Moira, was Aaron Stone.

Before making the decision that her hard-earned hangover would be best comforted in her own space, Laura took one last look at West Crumb's new attraction. Sure enough, it had begun to grow quite impressively, now standing several feet above even the tallest resident, with the crowd around it expanding equally as quickly.

It was tempting to stay and listen to the roaring of the protesters stopping any and all folk from approaching the fleshy pillar, but the ruckus was giving Laura a headache. Besides, she thought that if she wanted to watch a beanstalk grow, she'd read a fairy tale.

Because if she was honest, she was bored of the whole thing now.

Whatever it was, it *was* weird. But the fact it was making people weird and therefore even more annoying was what made Laura want to slink away, get under the duvet, and nap through the apocalypse. If, of course, it *was* the end of the world, because so far she had seen little sign that the Fleshberg and its sprouts had produced any threat against their way of life.

The most aggravating factor was working around the veins.

In her flat, Laura had to now navigate around protrusions that had popped up from her kitchen sink, bathroom sink, and toilet. The shower seemed to have been spared for now, and so she took advantage of this to feel vaguely normal again. A limbo through the stretched tendrils extending to the window followed, and Laura managed to force some water through the semi-blocked tap to brew up a coffee. It was no Joey special, but it would do.

As for Joey, he had also retired home. A quick fumble of her laptop, and the two were conversing once more through the medium of direct messages. A video call was touted, but Laura was deep in her onesie and had no intention of doing herself up. Not that she needed to with Joey, but it was good to maintain some decorum in these times.

The conversation had naturally led to Kevin and his current state of mind. Joey had been trying to contact him, but still had no luck. Now, though, there was fresh drama.

HE REALLY IS NOT WELL, Joey wrote.

TELL ME SOMETHING NEW.

NO, SERIOUSLY. HE'S BROKE.

HOW SO?

WELL, YOU KNOW THE GOD TEXTS?

STANDARD LOON.

YEAH. BUT HE'S NOT ALONE.

EH?

THE PROTESTORS.

WHAT ABOUT THEM?

WHAT DO YOU THINK?

-

The protestors were, indeed, not just there for the environmental aspects of the Fleshberg pillar.

They were quite passionate about it in general.

Ronald was finding this out through his wife, Moira. No matter how much he complained, pleaded, and reasoned, she would not be moved from her position protecting the pillar.

Not because it was like protecting a tree from being felled, that would have been a reasonable response for Ronald. No, Moira's motives were far more intriguing.

"It's alive."

"I… well, yes, I suppose it is…"

"Not like that, Ronald," Moira said. "It's actually alive. Like you and me."

"I don't think it's alive like me, Moira."

She paused, looking at her husband slightly confused. "Can you not hear it?"

"Hear what?"

Before Moira could clarify, Aaron arrived.

"Joining us, Ronald?"

"I was thinking more of breaking this up a little."

"Why?"

Ronald was surprised at Aaron's question. "Why do you think?"

"Don't you think it makes for a wonderful attraction?"

Looking at the fleshy, twisted sinew of the Fleshberg's pillar, Ronald didn't see the appeal.

"It's disgusting, Aaron."

"It's beautiful, Ronald. You just can't see that yet."

"Beau... what are you... what *is* going on?"

"Evolution," Aaron said.

"Evolution?"

"Both natural and spiritual."

As Ronald tried to take this in, the pillar's protectors started singing. What they were singing, he did not care to try and work out, but it sounded like a hymn.

Knowing that one could not get through to the devoted, he sighed and made his way back to the council offices. He would be having words with The Bureau that was for sure.

And as he left, Kevin stood by watching. Covered in something that was equal parts blood and equal parts something very slimy indeed.

The idea that the Fleshberg Pillar was now an attraction was odd, but not surprising, to Laura. After all, before that the only thing West Crumb had to offer in terms of tourism was its abundant supply of avant-garde roasting trays.

But there was an almost hypnotic appeal of the Fleshberg Pillar that drove people wild. All across social media, she read posts of people who had seen it, and demanded that they *had* to travel to her lowly little town as soon as possible. People of all ages were literally crying about how the Pillar was a thing of beauty, of how they needed to be near it, and so on.

It was a new type of madness, but not one that provided much amusement.

For Laura associated it immediately with Kevin and his manic texts. While she hadn't got as many as Joey did, they were still enough to showcase how upon seeing the Fleshberg for himself, Kevin had lost his mind.

Joey hadn't heard from him recently, which if she was honest Laura was glad of. But still, seeing people go crazy for the West Crumb Fleshberg Pillar was getting disturbing. Not least for the people who were already here.

One key figure that she saw interviewed far too often was Aaron Stone. Apparently, he was some sort of media guru for the council who was now running some sort of appreciation group toward the Pillar. With several clusters of beaming locals behind him, he told various news outlets how the Pillar was the biggest thing to hit West Crumb since that one reality show kid, and how he had big plans for it.

"West Crumb is now more than a student town, it's home to the Fleshberg," he said. "And by this time tomorrow, you're going to see it grow even more."

With this, the camera panned up to reveal that the Pillar was now past the rooftops of nearby buildings. You could still barely see the ends of the tendrils twitching at the top, but the eye was more drawn to the writhing, worm-like veins of the Pillar itself.

It made Laura feel sick, and yet she couldn't look away.

Which was lucky, as she caught sight of something.

She pinged Joey.

DID YOU SEE THAT?

WHAT?
ON 4 NEWS. THEY'RE AT THE PILLAR.

OK.

I SAW KEVIN.

For a moment, there was no answer, just the ominous text signalling that Joey was "typing".

Ultimately, the response didn't fit the wait.

SHIT.

Full of confidence and the type of bullish spirit that was befitting his generation, Ronald Pile made his way to the council offices to confront Treadwell and Keating. No longer would he be bullied or cajoled. He was going to take charge of this mess if they weren't, and prove that he was more than a council drone whose only use to them was as a "distraction".

When he arrived, the doors were locked. A notice on the door simply read:

CLOSED DUE TO THREAT

Feeling quite impotent, Ronald did the only thing he could do.

He went home.

Once there, he decided to treat himself. Seeing as Moira was more concerned with that monstrosity in the centre of town, he was going to order a takeaway, break out the good whisky, and sit around in his pants. He thought about having himself a tickle as well, but wasn't in the mood and instead decided to watch TV.

He ended up watching the world react to the West Crumb Fleshberg Pillar. While he would have preferred a bit of sport - or even his favourite game show - the Pillar was the talk of not just the nation, but also the world. Every channel dedicated some level of coverage to it, and it was easier to stick to one of the main news channels than be bombarded with ludicrous opinion pieces and wild speculation.

As his curry arrived and Ronald settled in his good chair, he watched as political pundits pontificated over the meaning of the Pillar, and whether early reports of the end of the world were presumptuous. Of course they were, Ronald had known that when it first kicked off. After all, it was his misquote that did the kicking.

Now he was getting the kicking as, naturally, the media blamed him for the panic.

He nearly threw a bhaji at the TV.

Before he wasted a good appetiser, his attention was drawn to the presence of Aaron Stone on his screen. The man hired to be his media messenger was now front and centre, the star of his own story. He answered questions about the Pillar, and spoke of how it was not the end of the world "as Mr Pile had claimed", but the beginning of a new one.

"I implore all to come to West Crumb," he said, staring deep into the camera, "and see the Pillar for yourself. Spend some time here, see what the Pillar gives you."

It was giving Ronald a headache, so he switched the TV off and ate the rest of his madras.

Everything was going faster than he could muster.

-

Kevin's cameo on the report had shaken Laura.

143

She had seen many people look a bit off. She even thought Kevin was more curious than most when she met him. As she had said many times before, Joey knew some interesting characters, but Kevin had seemed a different kind of interesting.

The dangerous kind.

And watching him almost drift through the crowd of Pillar enthusiasts in the centre of West Crumb was eerie. He seemed to be coated in something, like he'd bathed in margarine and cranberry juice. As Aaron Stone continued to sell the idea of West Crumb to those watching, Kevin slinked around behind him – not quite visible, but not inconspicuous to those that noticed.

HE WANTED ME TO JOIN HIM, Joey had messaged.

JOIN HIM WHERE?

OUT THERE. AT THE PILLAR.

SO YOU COULD JOIN THOSE LOONS?

YEAH. DON'T WORRY, I'M NOT.

GOOD TO KNOW.

BUT HE'S PLANNING SOMETHING.

WHAT?

HE DIDN'T SAY. BUT HE WAS EXCITED.

Laura didn't like the sound of that. Especially as Kevin didn't look excited on screen.

He looked mental.

19

Ronald got the call before his alarm went off.

In all honesty, he was surprised. He thought the rest of his days would be spent watching his wife go crazy over a weird tangle of... whatever they were, and the council being overthrown by The Bureau.

And yet, here he was, listening in as his presence was requested by the very party that cast him aside.

It was Treadwell, naturally, who had made the call. She had gone back to a tone of sunshine and roses, and was keen for Ronald to come in and be part of the team again. Or, at the very least, come in.

"Why should I?" he said.

"Because you're needed, Ronald."

"For more distractions?"

He grimaced as he heard Treadwell laugh. "No, no. No, we just need you here for certain matters."

"I'd like to know what those matters are before I make the effort."

"Does it matter?"

Ronald bit his tongue before entering any further wordplay.

"What is so important that you need me, someone who was so unimportant before, now?"

There was a brief murmur on the other end of the line before the sunny disposition suddenly turned cloudy.

"Pile, get to work," Keating said.

"Or what?"

"Or you're fired."

"So? Isn't it the end of the world? Oh no, wait, that was *me* saying that, wasn't it? It's not the end of the world. It's… barmy, is what it is."

There was silence on the other end of the line.

"We're yet to ascertain the status of the world and its end," Keating said.

As Ronald tried to process this comment, he was informed that a car would be arriving to pick him up and a coffee would be waiting inside. Just how he liked it.

It was all rather weird. But then again, it always was these days.

-

On the other side of West Crumb, Laura rose from the sofa where she'd fallen asleep, navigated the inconvenient strands from the Fleshberg that stretched across her flat, and managed to make a fresh batch of coffee. While this was the first morning where she hadn't consumed vast quantities of alcohol the night before, she still found herself with a pounding headache. For that matter, she also couldn't remember falling asleep.

Looking back over her messages with Joey, it seemed that neither did he.

YOU AWAKE?

Laura lazily typed back that she was, whilst eyeing how the previous conversation had ended abruptly with her typing KE.

SEEN THE NEWS?

The thought of further typing made Laura scowl, so she clicked the button to initiate a video call.

In a small box, the equally haggard Joey appeared.

"You look how I feel," she said.

"How much did you drink?"

"Nothing. You?"

"Not since… Well, not recently."

"OK. Mysterious hangovers aside, what's so important?"

"Turn the news on."

"Joey, I can barely tolerate the sound of your voice, let alone a reporter who's mainlining espresso. Just give me the cliff notes."

"OK. It's grown."

"What's grown?"

"Seriously?"

"My head hurts, OK? I'm not exactly operating on full cylinders here."

However, Laura did know that Joey was talking about the Fleshberg Pillar, and soon was informed that it had shot up in height. In fact, as Joey manoeuvred his laptop to the window, Laura was given a glimpse of how much it had actually increased.

It was quite impressive.

Joey's home was far from town, but even from his bedroom window you could see, protruding from where West Crumb's centre was, was a perfectly straight column stretching up into the clouds. Laura squinted at the image for a moment, ignoring Joey's queries if she could see enough, and decided to take a look for herself.

Following the path of her own invading tentacles, she poked her head out the window and down the street. Sure enough, towering over the rooftops was the Pillar. At this distance, she could see that not only was it taller, but it was also slightly thicker.

"What you thinking?" Joey said.

"You know that's a stupid question."

"Course I do, but I like to confirm. Meet me in town?"

"Sure. Wait! One other thing… have you heard from Kevin?"

Joey went silent. As she returned to her laptop, she saw Joey was back on his screen.

He didn't look good.

"Yeah."

"And?"

"I'll… I'll tell you when I see you."

Before questioning further, Laura instead noticed her phone on the floor, lit up with a single text.

From Kevin.

COME TO ME.

-

The car that picked Ronald up was more official than he was used to. The windows were tinted, the number plates were simply barcodes, and there was no brand to signify who had made it.

It certainly had a plush interior. He wasn't sure about the driver, though.

In fact, Ronald wasn't sure there was a driver.

Either way, the drive to the council offices was quicker than he expected. During the quick view of the news he had gathered, a substantial enclave was developing in West Crumb High Street, surrounding the Fleshberg Pillar. If he was honest, he was looking for Moira amongst the throng, but had to make do with Aaron Stone continuing his charm offensive with the media.

He wasn't the only one concerned by Aaron's pontificating. Upon entering the office, and being provided with the perfect cup of coffee, he saw that the remaining Bureau members – including

Treadwell and Keating – were watching the same footage. While he didn't catch the whispers between them, he did note their faces were more serious than he had seen before.

Of course, that snapped away once they realised he was there.

"Ronald! Glad you could make it," Treadwell said.

"You mean I had a choice?"

"No. Anyway, to business. We have someone we'd like you to meet…"

As swiftly as he had been fetched from his home, Ronald was strong-armed by two Bureau Agents, who carried him behind Treadwell and Keating. As they marched him through the corridors of the council he once called home, Ronald noted how empty it was.

It almost made him feel sad.

Such emotion was fleeting however, as the Agents directed him with a hard right into a conference room. In the past, the spacious room had mostly been home to various training seminars and ceremonial birthday celebrations.

Today, it was filled with maps, spreadsheets, and various other documents.

And instead of a middle-aged teacher at the head of the table, there was a person who made Ronald's head hurt.

"Mr Pile," Keating said, "meet Grounding Agent March Sunday."

20

For reasons neither could really explain, both Laura and Joey decided to skip meeting in the centre of West Crumb, and instead had positioned themselves on the top level of the nearby supermarket car park. The most obvious reason for their detour was the fact that the town centre now resembled a camping ground more than a high street, but there was also an unnerving feeling that Laura couldn't shake. She didn't know if it was the sight of Kevin or something else, but she had some relief in knowing Joey felt the same.

"Alcohol withdrawal," was his reasoning.

"I've had the hangover shakes, Joey," Laura said, sipping at her supplied coffee. "This is... different. Like when someone walks over your grave."

"If you will bury yourself on the high street..."

"That's an awful attempt at a joke."

"Yeah, well, my head hurts so..."

From their position they had a good view of not just West Crumb High Street, but also the Fleshberg Pillar, which had now grown immensely. It wasn't until they were in closer vicinity to the column of coiling veins that they could appreciate the sheer scale it had erupted to. Its trunk was now as thick as an old oak, still swirling with writhing tendrils, and its peak?

Well, that was what they were trying to find.

Joey had brought some binoculars with him, and was looking through them to get some idea of where the Pillar ended. But despite his best efforts, his view was thwarted by a thick gathering of clouds that had converged around it.

"Maybe we should hire a helicopter," Laura said.

Joey contemplated this, as she knew he would. Joey always had a knack for testing every avenue of something, no matter how absurd it was. Hire – or even steal – a helicopter? Seemed reasonable enough.

Until then, Laura took the binoculars and used them to scout the base of the Pillar. She scanned the crowds that had grown equally as large as the grotesque mass itself, looking for the eerie presence of Kevin.

Joey had shared his messages from their conspiracy-addicted acquaintance, and they were certainly an upgrade on the basic one Laura received. While he also asked Joey to COME TO ME, there were other messages that were more detailed. These spoke of FEEDING THE FLESHBERG, EMBRACING IT, and more curiously, CLIMB INTO ITS MAW TO SEE THE GLORY.

"What do you think the glory is?" Laura said.

"Not an open bar, that's for sure."

"Wasn't there rumours that the Fleshberg ate people?"

"I think it was more absorbing than eating."

"Whatever. But do you think that's what he meant? Or rather, 'means'?"

Joey thought about this as Laura carried on scanning the crowds.

"Oh yeah," Laura said, "what about his equally crazy friends?"

"Shit. Forgot about them…"

"Really? But they were so interesting…"

"No. I mean, he did mention them."

"And?"

Producing his phone from his pocket, Joey flicked through the messages until he reached the one he wanted.

Laura looked away from the binoculars and saw one word on screen.

SACRIFICES.

"Right," Laura said, sighing away any fears she now had. "I don't know what's worse, the fact he called them sacrifices, or the fact he ended it with a smiley face."

As Laura went back to scanning the crowd, Joey looked at his phone and shrugged. While she tried to locate their insane chum, the cogs in Joey's head turned a certain way causing a thought to suddenly pop.

"Laura, what if when he says 'climb into the maw' he doesn't mean the Fleshberg?"

"What else could he mean?"

Laura gave up on looking through the crowd, and turned her attention to Joey.

He was looking up at the Pillar, stretching into the clouds.

-

March Sunday was hard to look at.

After meeting the Grounding Agent, Ronald Pile immediately wondered if he needed his eyesight tested. Every time he looked at Sunday, the person was a constant blur; out of focus and seeming to shake against everything else around it. This shimmering appearance meant that he couldn't get a handle on whether Sunday was a man or a woman, old or young. Their face was always warping, with only their light grey eyes staying in place, and their voice simply an empty monotone.

Despite all this, Sunday was perfectly cordial. Unlike the passive aggression and aggressive aggression of Treadwell and Keating respectively, March Sunday didn't express any particular opinion of Ronald, which at least meant they weren't negative toward him. Instead, they invited him to take a seat, and began to talk about the Fleshberg.

"What do you know?" Sunday said.

"Err, that there's a big mass under our High Street?" Ronald said.

Sunday murmured to themselves, and noted this on a tablet. It must have been a modern model, as Ronald had never seen anything like it.

"May I ask you some personal questions, Mr Pile?"

"Sure?"

"Are you married?"

"Yes. Well, I think I am. My wife, Moira, has gone to worship that pillar…"

"Your wife's name is Moira?"

"Yes. Is that important?"

"Everything is important, Mr Pile," Sunday said.

As Ronald answered all the seemingly incidental questions Sunday came up with, he noted how the rest of The Bureau Agents – Treadwell and Keating included – seemed to treat this person with a certain kind of awe. Maybe it was because Sunday resembled a blur more than a person, and it was some sort of supernatural effect that made them special. Or something.

All Ronald knew was that their appearance gave him a headache.

"Last question," Sunday said, voice remaining as stoic as their expression, "what did you have for dinner last night?"

Ronald chuckled. "Does that matter?"

Sunday looked at him with their grey eyes. "Everything matters."

"OK. Well, I had a curry."

"What kind?"

"Madras."

"Onion bhajis?"

"Can't have a curry without them."

Ronald seemed pleased with this quip, but Sunday didn't share his enthusiasm. For the first time, the Grounding Agent looked slightly perturbed.

"I think that is everything," Sunday said, turning to Treadwell, "but I advise Mr Pile remain with us."

"Really?" Keating said.

"Yes. His presence adds 2.8% toward a positive outcome."

Ronald wasn't sure why being here with The Bureau had any statistical bearing on whatever outcome Sunday was talking about, but he was just pleased to be involved.

In fact, he listened with great interest as Sunday spoke to the Agents about many minor things, such as recent weather conditions, stock prices, and the names of those who went missing around the Fleshberg.

Then, he heard a name he recognised all too well.

"Do you have an Aaron Stone?"

"That prick?" Ronald said, before the Agents themselves could answer. "Don't worry about him."

Sunday paused and turned back to Ronald.

"Media advisor?"

"Yes. Well, he was. Now he seems to be the main publicist for that thing out there."

Once again, Ronald thought he saw Sunday grimace.

"Agent Sunday," Treadwell said, "what does that mean?"

With an almost ethereal air to them, Sunday moved around the long table they all sat around. They pushed around some papers and looked over a couple of articles before speaking.

"84%."

Ronald still didn't know what that meant, but he knew it wasn't good.

Because Treadwell nearly fainted, and Keating looked scared for the first time since arriving in West Crumb.

21

Sitting atop the car park, Laura had stopped scouting for any crazed conspiracy theorists they knew, and instead had turned her attention to Joey's phone. He had fired up the latest video from Aaron Stone, who was promoting the Fleshberg Pillar like it was the latest Wonder of the World.

"It isn't until you're in the presence of the Pillar," he said, "that you can appreciate it. And I know you folk out there *want* to appreciate it. So buy a ticket, get in your car, and come to West Crumb. We're all waiting for you."

The cheer that followed echoed over to the car park.

"Should we be scared?" Laura said.

"Probably," Joey said.

"I mean, when it was the end of the world, I was strangely fine with that. But now? Well, now you've just got nutters."

"Less predictable."

"Exactly. Crazy people are capable of anything. At least with the end of the world you know it's going to *be* something."

"In this case, a giant tumour under our town."

Laura laughed, but without too much mirth. As quickly as the apocalypse had been put on hold, it was now slowly raising its head again. Only this time, it wasn't some grotesque form of nature that threatened their way of life, but the human beings who saw it as some sort of glorious phenomenon.

It was, of course, very impressive. But the fanatical approach people had to it was what made Laura nervous.

Not to mention the fact that Kevin was now trying to find them. She had received a couple of texts enticing her to meet up, but Joey's phone was a constant buzz. It wasn't just messages, but missed calls and strange voicemails. They asked him where he was, when he was coming into town, and to call back.

Always in a tone best described as cheerfully empty.

The two of them knew they couldn't stay in the car park forever. They could go back to their homes but, since getting closer to where the Fleshberg Pillar was, the pains in their heads had abated somewhat.

Naturally, this led to some theorising. Radiation was the strongest contender, with Joey reasoning that the Fleshberg gave off some sort of radioactive pulse.

"So you think it was caused by radiation?" Laura said.

"What, the Fleshberg?"

"No, the recall on dark chocolate from the corner shop."

"I did enjoy that chocolate… but maybe? Like they said before, some toxic waste mixed with biological waste that came together to form the Berg."

"And the DNA?"

Joey just shrugged.

As they contemplated their next move, the sound of a small cheer was heard from the town centre. Laura got up first, taking Joey's binoculars, and looked to see what was causing the ruckus.

"Oh crap."

"What?" Joey said.

As he joined her from their vantage point, Laura passed him the binoculars.

"They're climbing the bloody thing."

Sure enough, through the lens, Joey saw a young man beginning to ascend the Pillar.

With the crowd below enthusiastically encouraging him.

-

Ronald didn't quite understand the relevance of what 84% meant, but then most things that The Bureau said between themselves made his head hurt.

Talking of which, Grounding Agent March Sunday was still looking over various reports, articles, and random documentation. Each time they found something they liked, they tapped it into their high-tech tablet and either looked happy or looked sad.

It was hard to tell the difference, if Ronald was honest.

He was enjoying being part of it all again, though. Fresh coffee was provided when required, and he even felt that Treadwell and Keating were treating him better. To be fair, they weren't treating him at all, fielding phone calls and providing Sunday with more information when they required it. But not being noticed was better than being noticed and called a moron.

Feeling a bit of a bond, he decided to try and make conversation with Sunday.

"So, what is a Grounding Agent?"

Sunday didn't answer, instead looking over some local sports results and keying them into his device.

"I suppose I am a bit of a Grounder as well," Ronald said, picking up the slang from one of the Bureau Agents. "I deal with parks. And gardens. The odd allotment."

"That is not the role of a Grounding Agent," Sunday said.

"Oh. Do you deal more with fields?"

This seemed to inspire a small grin from Sunday, and they took a moment from their study of random things to engage with Ronald.

"What do you know about The Bureau?" they said.

"Well I can tell you they've been quite rude to me," Ronald said, giving a conspiratorial side eye to Keating in particular.

"I watched your conference. You inferred that we do important things."

"Well, I would presume you do. All dressed in black suits and being hush, hush. Like those so-called 'men in black'."

Ronald laughed.

Sunday did not.

"You ask what a Grounding Agent is," they said, picking up a piece of paper from the table. "Would you still like to know?"

"Um…"

"I exist in every time, in every space. Every possible outcome of every possible decision in every possible point is in my view."

"Oh," Ronald said. "So you know the lottery numbers?"

"I know the lottery numbers."

"Care to share?"

"Ronald, there's an 86% chance you won't need them."

"You say that percentage thing…"

"I exist to see which timelines end, and how. I do this through analysis of variables and divergences. For example, on this piece of paper it says the price of your sandwiches here in the council cafeteria is £3.99. That tells me of an infinite number of decisions that were made to reach this point."

"So… the world is different based on the price of a ham-and-cheese?"

"Precisely."

166

"OK. Well, what about me?"

"Ronald Pile exists in many forms, some that would cause your brain to leak out your ear."

"I think I'm way ahead of you there."

"In some you're married to Moira. In others you're married to Greg, or Tina. Or maybe you never got married at all. Maybe you travelled. Maybe you died. Maybe you never were because your parents never met."

"Well this sounds depressing."

"For me to ascertain whether this dimension will survive what is happening with what you call the Fleshberg, I need to make sure variables are in place which could positively affect the future."

"And me being here is… positive?"

"Yes, Ronald."

This made Ronald feel good. Very good indeed.

"And who knows, maybe this conversation will also cause a positive effect," Sunday said, before looking at their device.

They shook their head.

"88%"

Suddenly, Ronald didn't feel as good. He decided to let Sunday keep working on, apparently, saving the world, while he took some time to clear his head.

He did wonder what would have made him marry Greg, though.

22

Watching the climber scale the Fleshberg Pillar was much like the old adage about car crashes; no matter how bad it got, Laura couldn't look away. The climber had no safety gear, no ropes to keep them from falling, and yet despite all this they were making impressive progress.

It was just terrifying to watch.

While she remained a captive audience, Joey was keeping on top of the news. Aaron Stone had continued his charm offensive, selling West Crumb as the place to be to enjoy this new, grotesque wonder of the world. It was eerie seeing how easily he hypnotised those watching, selling them the idea that the closer to the Pillar you were, the better your experience would be. There was no promise of fame, fortune, or anything else, just the opportunity to be in the proximity of the Pillar.

Aaron made no mention of the climber, though. While one reporter did try to steer the conversation to the young man scaling the Pillar, Aaron instead commented on how it was "only one of the many reasons to come to West Crumb."

"He really wants people to come here, doesn't he?" Laura said.

"Hell, I'm already here and I'm tempted," Joey said.

"If you go mental as well…"

Joey waved this notion away. "I'm more thinking I fancy a coffee."

"So go down there, mingle with the crazies?"

"They seem harmless."

"What about Kevin?"

To their unspoken relief, neither had heard from their conspiratorial chum recently. Laura hadn't seen him amongst the crowds below either, not since his brief cameo on TV. Wherever he was, he was lurking, and that didn't sit well with her.

Then again, she could do with a brew.

Feeling fearless against the swarm of Fleshberg acolytes, the two students left their station at the top of the car park, and ventured down into what was now West Crumb's Fleshberg hub. The town centre was less a shopping experience, and more of a festival; tents and small shantytowns had been constructed to allow the growing crowds there to be as close to the Pillar as possible. As the duo weaved through, Laura was glad of the fact that no one seemed to really notice they were there. Either they were enrapt at the sight of the Pillar, or talking excitedly to each other about the Pillar.

In a stroke of luck, the coffee shop was still open.

And business was naturally booming.

A couple of oat milk lattes later, Laura and Joey found a small area in which to sit down and take the sights in at ground level. The people here who were worshipping the Pillar moved breezily among each other, acting much like a commune. In a way it was quite lovely to see a community coming together, working as one in harmony.

Laura just wished it wasn't in thrall to a column made of fleshy tentacles.

She looked up, and saw that the climber was still making good progress. He had to be at least 30 feet from the ground by now, with no sign of slowing down. Using Joey's binoculars, she tried to get a closer glance.

Once focussed, Laura was sure that she saw the veins of the Pillar closing around the climber, almost pulling him up rather than assisting his climb.

It made her grimace.

"Do you really think we should stick around?" she said.

Joey just nodded, sipping away at his brew.

"OK, well shall we …?"

Before Laura could finish, the crowd around them went quiet.

At first she couldn't see why. But she *could* smell it. The aroma got worse as the crowd parted before them and a familiar figure lurched out.

"You came," Kevin said.

-

Every moment he remained in the office, drinking freshly brewed coffee that was supplied almost on the hour, Ronald Pile got the itch to be helpful. He didn't know how, but he felt that if anyone knew what he could do, it would be Grounding Agent March Sunday.

But Sunday was busy tapping at their device and managing The Bureau Agents, providing them with new and up to date information. Each new piece of paper or scrawled note was fed into the device, and provoked a reaction.

The good news was that, sometimes, the percentile went down. Ronald had no idea what was aiding this; one time he swore it was the type of tea available. But he was sure there was something he could be doing.

As Keating went to rush past, he put his hand up.

"Can I help?"

Keating stopped, looked at Sunday, and then back to Ronald.

"Stay there."

As he half jogged out the room, Ronald hoped this would mean that he was fetching him a task. No matter how small.

But Keating came back just as quick, and completely ignored him.

This was getting tiresome, so Ronald decided that the best way to be proactive was to do something on his own initiative. Excusing himself to go to the toilet – another piece of information that seemed to aid efforts by 1% - he instead snuck to his office and picked up the phone.

Aaron Stone's number was ingrained on his brain by now, and so when he finished punching it in and heard the successful dial tone, he felt pretty pleased with himself.

This doubled once Aaron answered.

"Who is this?" he said.

"Who do you think?" Ronald said.

"I don't know. It's an unknown number."

Ronald winced at this slight.

"It's Ronald Pile, Aaron. And I want to know what the Devil is going on."

"Ronald! So good to hear from you! Did you know your wife's here?"

"Um, yes. How do you know my wife?"

"Lovely lady. Makes nice towels. Very helpful in many ways. Anyway, why are you calling? Come on down, join the celebrations."

"Celebrations? What are you celebrating?"

"Why, the Pillar, of course. It continues to grow strong and thick, and people are loving it."

This statement caused Ronald to wince even harder.

"Aaron, why are you doing this?"

"Doing what?"

"Telling people to come to West Crumb."

174

"Tourism! You've got to strike while the iron is hot, Ronald. Otherwise, you've got a cold, wet iron."

"That doesn't make sense."

"Oh, it will if you pop on down. Come on, join the party."

"That doesn't answer my question," Ronald said, unaware of the *click* on the line. "Why are you so insistent that people come to West Crumb? And more specifically, that awful monstrosity?"

"Mon… do you mean the Pillar?"

"Well what other fleshy nightmares do you have down there?"

"Apart from the Fleshberg itself…"

"What is the point of this, Aaron?"

The line went quiet, with only the sound of the crowd behind Aaron; the low level chatter and community that one gets with large groups. After a few moments of hesitation, he spoke up again.

"I just want people to come to the Pillar."

"Why?"

"I… don't know."

"Is that why you leaked the footage?"

"I don't know."

"And did those press releases?"

"I don't know."

"Aaron, what is going on?"

Once again, there was silence.

"I'm sorry, Ronald. I have to go," Aaron said, his voice flat and less hyper than before.

As the dial tone buzzed in Ronald's ear, he looked up to see Agent Sunday standing there, device in hand.

"82%," they said. "Not bad."

He didn't know how, but Ronald had actually helped.

23

To put it mildly, Kevin was disgusting.

Laura thought he had looked horrific on camera, but now he was standing in front of her, she could see and *smell* the full layers of grotesque that coated his stagnant clothes. There were signs of old sweat and grease upon his skin, but also some strange sheen that was thick and reminded her of the stuff babies were covered in when they were born.

Then there were also the multiple dark red stains splattered randomly upon his clothes.

While she was managing to just about keep her panic in check, Joey was maintaining a better façade of calm. If Laura didn't know better, she'd think that he had been hypnotized by the glory of the Fleshberg, but as devout as Kevin seemed, he lacked the charisma that Aaron Stone had.

Indeed, as he guided them through the crowds, Kevin babbled on about the Fleshberg and the Pillar that had grown from it. He seemed anxious, almost manic, as he spoke about how it was a miracle of nature, and would signal the next step.

"The next step in what?" Laura said.

He looked at her, eyes nearly bulging out their sockets.

"Everything."

It was immediately obvious to both Laura and Joey that Kevin had gone from conspiracy theorist to full-blown acolyte. He would pause at moments to stand in awe of the Pillar, and look up into the clouds where it seemed to end. He was now past creepy and into the realms of absolutely terrifying, but Laura knew that they couldn't do anything about it.

For one, the commune around them was far too large.

The people who had made the pilgrimage to the Pillar, and now camped around the base, all seemed to treat Kevin with a certain respect. Nobody really spoke to him, but if he spoke to them they listened intensely. Not that he spoke much, instead trying to ingratiate Laura and Joey with groups. He'd introduce random people here and there, and Laura would politely smile and wave, but apart from that there was no real attempt by him to engage.

He just seemed to imprint some sense of reverence in them.

Of course, Laura felt that this illusion of a joyous community would soon fade away and reveal something very ugly underneath. Sure enough, over by one of the local pub chains, a small group were huddled and muttering to themselves. Laura and Joey watched as Kevin made his excuses to break away and see what the drama was.

"I don't like this," Laura said.

"It's certainly… weird."

"That's putting it mildly. I feel like we're in Jonestown."

"Nice. Where do you think the Kool Aid is?"

179

Laura looked up at the Pillar.

Kevin spoke. "Everyone! We have another who wishes to ascend."

The way he said this made it sound like a gift, but Laura wasn't sure the young woman he pulled alongside him was 100% invested in the idea. Sure, she was smiling and waving to the crowd that cheered her on, but as Laura had always been able to tell, the eyes told a very different story.

They were scared.

Now she thought of it, Laura had no idea what happened to the previous climber. Since being invited into the commune by Kevin, their attention had been cleverly dragged away from the scene. Now they had a front row seat to this bizarre ceremony, and stood there as Kevin led the woman to the base of the Fleshberg Pillar, taking a moment to reassure her.

"You're doing a great thing," he said, before gesturing to the Pillar.

Despite a moment of hesitation, she began to climb.

As the crowd of Fleshberg enthusiasts chanted their support, Laura saw up close how, when the woman gripped the Pillar, the tendrils looped around her hands and feet to secure her. From deep within the centre of the twisted veins, a longer, thicker vine looped out and wrapped around her waist. Even if she wanted to, there was no way she could break away from the Pillar.

180

The only way to escape was up.

Wherever that went.

-

The moment of joy caused by Ronald's call to Aaron didn't last long.

As soon as The Bureau Agents gathered back into the conference room, with Ronald in tow feeling like the cock of the walk, Grounding Agent March Sunday looked at their device and suddenly took a breath.

The other Agents knew not to ask, because it was painfully obvious.

"92%" Sunday said.

As the Agents fell back into a flurry of work, Ronald wondered what the Hell just happened. After all, only seconds before he had temporarily saved the world.

"I thought you said it was 82%?"

Sunday just grunted a confirmation.

"So what happened?"

"Unforeseen circumstances," Sunday said.

"Unforeseen... what does that mean?"

"Existence is chaos, Mr Pile. As I've told you, the slightest twitch can cause ramifications that are beyond your understanding."

"A butterfly flaps its wings, yes, I've heard of that nonsense."

"In this case, a butterfly hasn't flapped. It has grown to the size of a continent and eaten the people there."

For a moment Ronald struggled with this statement.

"Has that actually happened?" he said.

"Not here," Sunday said.

That didn't help Ronald's understanding.

"From what we can tell, while Aaron Stone has been nullified, another element has been introduced," Treadwell said, looking over a laptop showing CCTV of West Crumb High Street.

Sunday looked over some reports while Ronald struggled where to concentrate.

"Do we have a census?"

"We can do a mobile check."

"What's a mobile check?" Ronald said.

"We send out a ping and find out every person within a calculated radius," Treadwell said, almost as if Ronald should have known this.

"You can do that?"

"We're The Bureau, Ronald. We can do anything."

Truly, this had been evident since Treadwell and Keating first walked into the offices of West Crumb's council offices. They walked with a confidence and power that he hadn't seen even from the highest level of local MP. It was what made the fact that they were scurrying around that little bit more concerning.

Even as he tried lightening the mood, it only served to darken the room.

"If you can do anything, surely you can save the world," he said.

Nobody responded.

Ronald just treated himself to a nervous laugh.

"OK, ping results are in," Treadwell said, pointing at Sunday's device. Sure enough, the data had transferred and Sunday was now looking over it all, trying to ascertain the situation and how it affected the percentile. As Ronald watched all this happen, he wondered if he was still needed here.

Sunday made a noise. One that, given their nature, was hard to discern whether it was good or bad.

"Everything alright?" Ronald said.

The Bureau Agents all waited for Sunday's response.

"95%"

Ronald spoke for everyone when he swore very quietly and very sadly.

24

One had to admire the community spirit that had erupted around Laura at that moment. Crowds of people, from all different walks of life, came together to cheer and celebrate with an unfettered joy not seen since the last West Crumb Craft Fayre.

And yet, what they were celebrating was the ascent of a fellow local climbing up a pillar made entirely of winding, flesh-like veins that had sprouted from a gigantic tumour in the sewers below.

It was a curious perspective, for sure.

That wasn't the only thing that bothered Laura. It wasn't until Joey pointed it out to her that she realised; since entering the commune of Fleshberg fanatics, they were no longer standing on good old-fashioned tarmac. Instead, the road and pavements of West Crumb High Street had been replaced by a mish-mash of carpets and rugs acquired from various local stores, covering the hundreds of tendrils that had crawled from the various drains, faucets, and assorted outlets. It wasn't until the climb began and the ground started squirming that the change was noticeable.

While unspoken, both Laura and Joey knew that they were in a very disturbing place.

Adding to that feeling was Kevin, who stood next to them as they watched the woman continue to 'climb'. Instead of cheering her

185

on with the crowd, he just watched, with the sort of intensity Laura had felt was creepy when they first met.

Naturally, it all added to the ever-growing feeling of getting-the-Hell-out-of-there.

As the climber began to fade from view, Kevin turned to Laura and Joey expecting a reaction. There was plenty that the two of them could provide, and Laura did consider maintaining the same politeness that she had adopted upon their first encounter. But she also felt that, given the situation, white lies were no longer acceptable.

Then again, she also knew not to shake a hornet's nest. Especially when you're inside one.

"Interesting," she said.

"Isn't it? Such an honour to be chosen," Kevin said.

Joey remained silent as Laura smiled, nodded, and tried to think of some phrase or response that would both placate Kevin as he spoke, - enrapt by the Fleshberg Pillar - and not aggravate. He had gone from being a harmless nut to someone who had crossed the line of crazy into the darker areas. The calmness in his voice, the way he waxed lyrical, it all added to an unnerving feeling that did not dwindle the longer they stood there.

Just as the excuses in her brain were considered and discarded, Laura saw a person approach. Unlike most of the people in the Fleshberg Commune, he was smartly dressed, neatly put together, and may even have moisturised.

"Kevin, we need to talk."

"Aaron. How is everything," Kevin said, before introducing Aaron Stone to Laura and Joey. They both continued their routine of smiling politely while allowing the two men to talk.

"Can we go somewhere quiet?"

"Quiet? What do you mean?"

"Somewhere we can talk openly," Aaron said, looking around at the crowds of followers.

"Aaron, you can speak openly here…"

The way the words trailed off made Laura feel even more uneasy. She joined Aaron's gaze at looking over the crowd, and saw among those that continued their business, others gave fleeting glances toward them.

"It's just… I have… I don't know."

"Don't know?" Kevin said.

Laura watched Aaron nervously consider his words, before giving in to himself.

"What is all this? What are we doing?"

Kevin didn't say anything, but Laura believed his fixed smile was wavering.

"It all seems a bit…" Aaron laughed, more nervous than amused. "It seems a bit strange?"

"Strange?"

"Yeah. As in, *what the Hell*? We've discovered a giant fleshy mass in the sewers that's now spewed hundreds of these... tentacle things, and we've just accepted that?"

Kevin remained silent, but Laura saw his eyes speak very loudly.

"And... and I know I've been telling people to come visit, in the name of tourism and interest... but why? There's no financial benefit to it. People aren't spending money. They're just... camping. Here. Like demented hippies."

The eyes of the crowd were becoming more focussed on the discussion between Kevin and Aaron, with Laura's sense of unease growing by the second. It would be bad form to just run, but there was plenty of merit in slowly edging away.

If there were any gaps in the crowd to do so, of course.

"Aaron, you sound troubled," Kevin said.

"I'm not troubled, I'm just... confused, that's all."

"You need answers."

Aaron didn't respond to this, the words unable to pop out of his open mouth no matter how much he shook his head.

"Maybe you need to see things up close."

With that, Aaron's bobbling ceased.

"Up close?"

188

"Yeah," Kevin said, lips smiling but eyes betraying a very different expression.

Laura did not like it.

"Or maybe I just need a break?"

"Nonsense. Let's have some of the people here take you down."

It had been as insidious as every other aspect of the commune; Laura noted how several people had silently arrived close to Aaron. Not just any folk, either - strong men who looked like the type who posted selfies of themselves at the gym. The kind that always seemed to bother Laura on social media.

Their expressions made her glad she'd never responded.

"Kevin..."

No more was said between the two as Aaron was calmly, yet absolutely forcefully, pulled into the crowd. As he vanished amongst the pockets of people chatting, gossiping, doing chores and generally enjoying the communal aspect of it all, Laura felt Joey close to her ear.

"Think we need to go?"

She nodded very slowly.

-

Things had become equally as tense in the offices of the West Crumb Council.

Ronald Pile knew that 95% wasn't very good, but he had no idea how not very good it was until the people from The Bureau set about packing up their equipment and making plans to leave as soon as possible.

He tried to reassure himself that they were just preparing for a lower scale operation, and that all the computers, devices, and unknown tech they were filing out the door were no longer applicable to the overall situation.

Yet, as much as he tried smiling his way through it, he was aware of how Treadwell and Keating were in serious conversation with Sunday.

Still, he couldn't just stand there like a lead balloon amongst the maelstrom. As the current – and seemingly only – representative of the West Crumb Council, he was allowed to be privy to the latest goings on.

It would be rude to just interrupt, so he casually stood next to the three agents and bided his time to interject.

When that time didn't come, he resorted to a series of coughs and other sounds to announce his presence.

It wasn't well received.

"Are you still here?" Treadwell said. It seemed like her ongoing charm had now been disposed of, and the reality of a woman who was Serious Business was in place permanently.

"Well…"

"Well? Is that all you can say? Well?"

Keating was still an arsehole, it seemed.

As Ronald stammered through the barrage of stern questions, Sunday watched on. Ronald had found the ambiguous Agent disquieting since they met, but Sunday's emotional indifference, especially now, made them even more jarring. In fact, after peppering Ronald with casual insults and passive aggressive demands, Treadwell and Keating seemed equally as shook when Sunday spoke up.

"You did all you could, Mr Pile."

"Did I?"

"Of course. Your actions may have in fact done some good."

Ronald nodded at Treadwell and Keating as if to say that he told them so.

He hadn't, of course.

"Ultimately, it was futile," Sunday said.

"Oh."

"But such is the nature of circumstance. The Universe continues to be chaotic, dominos fall as expected. Actions beget consequences, and so on."

The whimsical way Sunday spoke put Ronald strangely at ease, but he still felt very concerned about the fact that they were likely facing the end of the world. How could Sunday be so calm about such a thing?

Ronald realised he had said that last part out loud.

"When you've seen as many apocalypses as I have, Mr Pile, a world ending becomes as mundane as a light breeze."

"That's… depressing."

Sunday shrugged. "That's existence."

"Fair enough."

As Treadwell and Keating made their excuses, and the hive of activity around Ronald seemed to become less and less, he felt powerless to do anything. The consequences, it seemed, were so much more than he could influence, and in the end he was just another person, standing in an office with a figure who seemed to shimmer in and out of the very existence that they had explained was so fickle.

As Sunday began to leave as well, Ronald had one last question.

"What now?"

Sunday turned around, seemed to smile, and nodded to Ronald.

"Prepare for the end."

25

In theory, making your way through a crowd is a simple premise. After all, it merely involves the polite manoeuvring around people, gliding through available pockets of space when they present themselves. What could possibly go wrong?

Like most theories, everything. Everything can go wrong, and invariably does very quickly if one is not careful.

You could find that those pockets of open space are, in fact, a lie that will suck you deeper into the living throng you are trapped within. No matter how hard you twist and weave and squeeze, the mass of the crowd melds together into a fleshy congregation where even air struggles for room. Obviously, over time and with an injection of aggression, a person can find their way to the sanctuary of the crowd's edge, but history does dictate many instances where, no matter how hard those stuck within the human hive tried, their fate was ultimately sealed.

While their position was less fatal, it was no less traumatic for Laura and Joey. For what seemed far longer than it should have been, they smiled and apologised and forced their way through the gigantic moss of the commune, edging further and further from the Fleshberg Pillar that was their epicentre. Kevin had not seen them leave, but neither could put this down to luck or circumstance. In the end, Joey summed it up best.

"Even the best cult leaders can't watch every follower."

"Yeah, but then they don't need to," Laura said, excusing herself through another throng of Fleshberg enthusiasts.

"How so?"

"It's a cult, Joey, they don't exactly leave outsiders be."

As she said this, Laura looked to see a middle-aged man looking at her. His expression didn't *suggest* he was offended, but then again it was hard to tell these days.

With each sway and bob, the duo hoped to reach the edge of the commune. However, while it seemed to only be small from their first view, now they were deep inside it became more of a labyrinth. They had been using West Crumb's church steeple as a guide, but every time they thought they were close, they looked up to see they had gone in a completely different direction.

This led to Laura's suspicion that they weren't in control of their own movements. That, somehow, the crowd was moving them.

With that thought in mind, she sat down on some recently uncovered steps to take a moment.

Joey didn't argue.

"Thirsty?"

They turned to see a pink-haired lady offering them a bottle of water each. It wasn't until she made the offer that Laura realised how parched she was, and took the water with plenty of gratitude.

"Are you new?"

Laura had a mouth full of aqua, so Joey responded for the both of them. "In a way."

This amused Pink Hair. Neither was sure why.

"It's exciting, isn't it?" she said. "Nothing like this ever happens in West Crumb."

"I don't think this sort of thing happens in most places," Laura said, again provoking a series of titters.

"When I first heard about it, I was worried. It's hard not to be when the man from the council mentions the end of the world. But now I see it for what it really is and that's very reassuring, you know?"

Joey nodded, but Laura wasn't in an entertaining mood.

"It's still the end of the world, though."

"Oh my dear, only in a figurative sense. It's like a chrysalis. A rebirth."

"More like an afterbirth."

"Sorry?"

"Nothing," Laura said, realising she had spoken out loud. "So how did you find out that it was... reassuring?"

"How do you think?" Pink Hair said, gesturing to the crowd around them.

"OK, but did you just stroll on down and pitch a tent? Or..."

196

"Oh I had friends already down here. They're like me, a bit of a questioner. One of their daughters ended up going down in the sewer with Him."

The way Pink Hair emphasised the H caught Laura's ear.

"Him?"

"Kevin."

Immediately, Laura's *OH SHIT* alarm began ringing. Loudly.

"You know Kevin?"

"We all know Kevin," Pink Hair said, amused by the concept that someone wouldn't. "He's the one closest to the Fleshberg."

"We noticed he was a bit mucky," Joey said.

"That's not muck, my dear, that's his baptism. My friend's daughter wasn't so lucky, but Kevin? Well, you've met him I assume."

"We're on… terms," Laura said.

"He's doing wonderful things. And that other boy, Aaron? He's helping spread the word."

"I don't think for much longer."

"And when it is time, it will happen."

Laura exchanged a quick look with Joey.

"What will happen?"

"He will give passage to The One."

The reverence and consonant emphasis once again caught Laura's ear, and she didn't like it anymore than referring to Kevin with a capital pronoun.

So, with her best effort of politeness, she thanked Pink Hair for the water and ushered Joey up. Then, she decided to take a punt.

"How does one leave the commune? You know, for reasons?" Laura said.

"Oh, you want to leave?"

"Just to get some supplies."

"Well, we have supplies here."

"Oh, these are special supplies. They're… gluten free."

Pink Hair tried to continue her argument to stay, but instead nodded in understanding. She pointed to her right and suggested the two make their way past the tents with the green flag on it, before taking a right at the one with the red flag.

"They like flags," she said, as if that meant something.

Laura didn't care; what it meant to her and Joey was that they had a way out of there. And after passing the green flag and taking a right at the red flag, they were finally out.

It was the other side of West Crumb, but at least it wasn't full of tent-dwelling cultists awaiting The One.

Whatever that was.

-

Now the boxes were packed and the files all neatly filed away, Ronald Pile was finally alone in the office.

After speaking with Grounding Agent March Sunday, it all happened in the blink of an eye; one moment The Bureau were there, and now they weren't.

"Hello?" Ronald said, just in case.

The response was a resounding silence.

There was literally nothing left. No paperwork, no stationary with a Bureau logo on it. Just empty offices, void of any life except the hum of the fluorescent lights and the strange feeling of monitors in their technological half-life of stand by.

Surely this couldn't be it, Ronald thought.

So he picked up the phone.

At first he didn't know who to call, content listening to the drone of the dial tone. Then, he thought of calling Aaron Stone, but was swiftly told that he was out of service. He then tried calling Moira at home, before remembering after a few feeble rings that she was now stationed at the Fleshberg Pillar.

Naturally, his next step was the Mayor.

Mayor Hassan was a private man who, in reality, held a mostly ceremonial role. But there had been the odd occasion where his finger was near the pulse, and maybe he could provide some direction for Ronald in these confusing times. As the phone rang, and Ronald looked at the blank walls where maps once stood, he felt a growing sense of dread.

"Hello?"

"Hello, Mayor?"

"Speaking."

"Excellent. My name is Ronald Pile and…"

"Who?"

"Pile. Ronald Pile. I work for the council?"

The other end of the phone was silent.

"I've been working with The Bureau on this whole Fleshberg thing?"

Still silence.

"Are you still there?"

"Why are you calling, Ronald?"

That voice did not belong to Mayor Hassan. In fact, Ronald had no idea who that voice belonged to, leading to the obvious step.

"Who is this?"

"Why does it matter?"

"Because I was speaking to the Mayor," Ronald said.

"You don't need to."

"I don't… who is this?"

200

"We've already dealt with things. Just relax and do something else."

"We… wait. Am… am I talking to The Bureau?"

"The Bureau doesn't exist, Ronald. They never did. They never came to West Crumb, never tried to study the Fleshberg, and never came to the conclusion that it represented an Eldritch Threat."

"That sounds like some very specific things that never happened."

"Ronald, you were told to just prepare for the end, so go do that. Buy yourself a nice steak, maybe a prostitute or five, we don't care. All we care about has passed, everything else is just time."

Ronald was stunned. Here he was, trying to talk to the Mayor and instead just being instructed by someone who was very obviously from The Bureau – despite them apparently not existing – telling him to embrace the apocalypse with a good meal and plenty of illicit sex.

Well, obviously this person didn't know Ronald Pile.

"Now listen here, you," he said, "I want answers, and I want them sharpish. You don't think you lot can just come in here, fanny about, and then bugger off without so much as a thank you. I helped you lot out, so I deserve a little bit of respect, even if I didn't get it before. After all, Agent Sunday said I helped postpone the inevitable."

Saying that out loud made Ronald realise it wasn't as impressive as he thought.

What was worse was that while he had been saying this, the phone had been disconnected.

In fact, everything had been disconnected. There was no phone service, no internet, and even the reception on his mobile had been wiped out.

All Ronald had was the hum of the lights and feeling that someone had left a monitor on.

Maybe he would get himself a steak after all.

26

Despite all that was growing – figuratively and literally – in the centre of West Crumb, the night ended up being a rather passive one. After escaping the crowd of Fleshberg cultists, Laura and Joey had scavenged various snacks of questionable goodness from empty shops, as well as several large bottles of booze, and made the decision to camp at Joey's.

This had suited Laura; the idea of going back to her flat, now filled with several flaccid veins from her faucets, didn't exactly appeal. While the tendrils from the Fleshberg seemed benign, she still wasn't keen sleeping next to one as it pulsed whatever was inside it out the window.

As for going to the toilet? Well, she missed the portaloos.

And so it was that Joey's house – far from the town centre and only mildly invaded by fleshy strings – was to be their last bastion. The home in which they would drink merrily, eat disgustingly, and recall all sorts of tales that had occurred during their brief, but close, friendship.

Not that they knew this would be the final night, but neither of them could shake a growing sense of foreboding. As jovial tipsiness crawled into melancholic inebriation, they both felt that whatever was happening with the Fleshberg wouldn't end well.

And that ending was due very soon.

-

After a steak and several large tumblers of whisky, Ronald Pile felt a little bit better about the whole situation. Yes, The Bureau had vanished and left behind not just an empty office, but also a lack of all hope, one still had to try and look on the bright side.

He didn't even have to pay for the steak.

Ronald knew that he was just fooling himself, though. Every positive thought that was spun and laid out as a sheet, was ultimately a temporary plaster on the insane situation that West Crumb had found itself in. No matter how hard he tried, the idea of seeing the best in this situation was tricky to say the least. After all, it involved a giant fleshy tumour in the middle of years of detritus. Which then seemed to eat people and sprout thousands of tentacles. Which *then* wrap around themselves to create some sort of grotesque pillar that stretches into the sky through clouds that no one can see past. And after *all of that*, people start worshipping the damn thing, including his *wife*, and...

Nope. It couldn't be done.

In fact, one thing had haunted Ronald, and he didn't realise it until he sat in his chair quietly, sipping away at yet another whisky. When he had spoken to Aaron Stone - a man who seemed to embrace the Fleshberg and all its opportunities - his questions had seemed to break something in him. Personal armour, perhaps made of delusion, which had crumbled apart once the reality of the Fleshberg and its horrific nature was exposed to him. It gave him a sudden sense of self-awareness.

Or rather, fear.

To muse on such things was not for Ronald Pile, though. That was why he was drinking so heavily. Yes, he felt more impotent than ever before, personally as well as professionally, but he was also scared.

Although not alone in this feeling, he felt nightmares etching harder and deeper into his brain, and that sleep would only give them a louder platform to scream from. Therefore, the less time spent in a sort of waking slumber, the better.

Like many of those who weren't in awe of the Fleshberg, lashings of alcohol seemed to be the best way to combat such terrors.

-

With loaded backpacks and only the mildest hangovers, Laura and Joey prepared to head back to the West Crumb centre. Although to call it the West Crumb Town Centre was to give it the moniker of a past era. It was now less a high street and more a hub for those who were acolytes to the Fleshberg Pillar. No more commerce or street markets, just mindless devotion to thousands of fleshy strings wrapped around each other.

But it was the place to be, if not for the rapture that others seemed to have about the Fleshberg, but to get a better idea of what was going on. There had been thoughts of leaving West Crumb entirely - grabbing a train and making their way far across the globe enough to never see a tendril again. Any resistance had long left West Crumb, and so both Laura and Joey were more confident in gaining some sort of exit.

However, while the mysterious Bergers had gone, the tendrils hadn't. Looking off a bridge, the two silently took in the sight of dozens of Fleshberg veins wrapped around the tracks and breaking them apart.

"Looks like the warning was right," Joey said.

"What warning?" Laura said.

"When I told people I was coming to West Crumb to study, some said you end up staying here. Like it was a residential black hole, consuming all who step within its boundaries."

"Bit much, isn't it?"

"Yeah, but the same basic idea rings true."

"Which is?"

"You can never leave."

Joey nodded down the hill, and from where the two of them stood they could see the main road across the valley that led to the motorway. Sure enough, makeshift barricades had been made using various cars and lorries, crunched together in a bizarre union of mechanics and – of course – tendrils.

Laura nodded to herself, and simply sighed.

"Guess we're fucked then."

"Pretty much."

"Well, may as well see how we're going to be fucked."

The skip in their step was drenched in sarcasm, but as the duo sauntered downhill, they took a look toward their destination.

A place where a huge sinewy pillar stretched into the sky without end.

-

Hangovers for the young are simple inconveniences, but for the middle-aged like Ronald, they were knives dragged across your nervous system.

It took him three attempts to open his eyes, and two further attempts to get out of bed. There had been vomiting, and a shower that was best described as miserable, but he was now fresh, dressed, and ready to go about his day.

Of course, he no longer had a day. He no longer had anything. He was just a man without a mission.

Sure, he could go back to the council offices, but to what end? The complete hollowing out of its facilities – from lockers to the actual internet – meant it would be a task in pointlessness. Normally, he'd go for a walk with Moira, but she was now entrenched in the craziness of the Fleshberg commune.

The only other option was to meander around town, but given most of that was commune and the rest was paved with slithering appendages, there wasn't much appeal.

So Ronald turned on the telly to watch the news.

Of which there was none.

Well, there probably was news, but Ronald would be none the wiser. All his TV now broadcast was the hypnotic scrawl of static as it tried to locate any sort of signal. He did wonder if this was another move of The Bureau, in order to cut West Crumb and its curiosities from the rest of the world, but what did it matter?

As far as Ronald knew, the rest of the world knew anyway. And wanted in.

Maybe.

Ronald really didn't know anymore.

To call it depression was to label how he felt with a large brush soaked in black. He didn't feel depressed, or at least not how he perceived depression to be felt. Ronald just felt... hopeless. Lost. Stuck in a place where no matter what he did, his actions would make no ripple on the larger picture. He had done something, but as Agent Sunday of The Bureau had told him, it meant little more than a minor percentile to the larger sum.

In fact, the idea of the Fleshberg made Ronald feel even smaller. For it was a curiosity, an unknown that he couldn't easily put into a category. Normally, any sort of new flora or fauna would be neatly filed away in a little box for him to manage moving forward, but this had not only been an unusual entity, it was something that destroyed everything in his life.

As he thought that, a spark flashed in Ronald's mind. It should be said at this point that when one is in a state of utter desolation, the ideas that gain strength are normally not good ones at all. In fact, their very rationality is on par with thinking one can control their bowel needs through sheer will alone.

Eventually, shit will occur.

And in Ronald's mind, shit did indeed start to flow.

The Fleshberg had destroyed his life. So, naturally, he would destroy it.

It made perfect sense. In a way.

27

The concept of normality was, in truth, a lost one these days. No one thought this more than Laura. But then again, her generation were used to the absurd and obscene breaking out from the comfortable sheen of life. To the outside layman, the fact that she had grown up through recessions, war, the rise of social media, and the post-fact ideology meant that things like the Fleshberg were par for the course.

So, as her and Joey entered the commune in West Crumb's centre once again, the atmosphere of cult-like community and a general hivemind was a new normal that had transitioned seamlessly from the old ways. It just consisted mainly of folk in tents, praising a grotesque pillar that stretched beyond the clouds.

Not to mention the entrance to the sewers.

Laura hadn't given that much thought at first, but as she and Joey weaved through the friendly people offering things they mostly ignored, she was taken by the queue that filed into the manholes. There were only a few on the high street – probably no more than five – and the ones directly above the Fleshberg had already been destroyed by the writhing mass of tendrils that had burst forth. But each one was manned by one or two people happily guiding others downward toward the underground waste. Some looked delighted to be going, while others did not strike Laura as true believers.

Not that her and Joey were either. The deeper they got into the dense crowd of fanatics, the more they got the sense of not belonging. There seemed to be a more primal way of life here now, more focused on devotion to the Fleshberg than basic things like sanitation or general hygiene.

Joey summed it up best.

"They do say cleanliness is next to godliness."

"So... by being filthy they're what? Showing their place?"

"Something like that?"

"That's a clunky theory."

Joey simply waved his hand in defiance. He knew what he meant.

After all, this was a cult.

The clusters of folk closest to the Fleshberg Pillar seemed to just merge in awe of it. As the veins continued to wrap themselves around the fleshy structure, making it thicker and stronger each moment, they cooed and moaned in an almost uncomfortable manner. Laura could see them caressing the mass and applying ointments and other assorted mixtures to it, treating it in spite of how they were treating themselves. It was behaviour that, on a base level, didn't make much sense.

But as Laura had already postulated herself, this world no longer made sense. It was just a tyre fire soaked in madness.

A thought that happened to coincide with them finding Kevin.

He was still filthy; his rotting clothes and grey skin covered in the glimmering sheen they had seen him coated in before. It was part of a growing ensemble, however, as much like his fellow followers his hygiene had long since departed and his body was now showing the effects. His hair was matted and clumps had departed his scalp, and what teeth hadn't abandoned ship were an exotic colouration of yellow and black. Rather than the vaguely plump nutter they had met in the pub not a few days prior, he was beginning to look gaunt; any fat in his body since eaten away leaving behind an empty shell.

Except, he wasn't empty. Oh no. While his physical body was nothing short of a mess, Laura saw in his eyes that his brain was still as wild and vigorous as ever.

"You came back," he said upon seeing Laura and Joey.

"We couldn't stay away," Laura said. "Apparently this is the place to be these days."

"You have no idea."

Kevin turned away, waving for the two to follow. They were led through the crowd and, curiously, away from the pillar. As his followers parted for Kevin to drag himself through, Laura noted how the various people were staring at her in a kind of reverence. It was the same look she had got from various drunken men on a night out.

Much like then, she didn't like it.

Soon enough, though, they arrived at the point Kevin was leading them to. It was a nice, well-kept tent fit for a decent sized family, and was decorated in a manner that clashed with the basic environment around them. Candles shimmered, coloured throws hung carefully, and there was an actual bed inside.

As nice as this was, it didn't make Laura feel any less suspicious.

"You like it?" Kevin said. His attention focussed more toward Laura than Joey.

"Will we both fit?" Joey said.

Kevin laughed. The sound made Laura feel sick.

"I've got a special quarter for you across the way, Joe."

"Why can't he stay here?" Laura said.

"Why would he?"

Laura went to answer, but Joey patted her on the shoulder. Everything was going to be fine, they just had different areas for some reason.

Of course, the reason was glaringly obvious, but when surrounded by mad people, it was always best to just play along.

As Kevin led Joey off, Laura watched her friend be consumed by the crowd. She stood there for a moment, wondering what to do next.

And the dozens surrounding her seemed to be waiting for that as well.

-

Now, as the Fleshberg Fanatics showed, sanity was in short supply in West Crumb these days. One could easily allow themselves to be mentally broken in all sorts of ways, and it was a crapshoot as to how they would be built back up. Most had used the Fleshberg and the tower it had created as their own philosophical nucleus, while Ronald Pile had gone down a different route.

It would be easy to argue that his sudden epiphany to destroy the Fleshberg was a left field choice, but then one would have to look over the life of Ronald Pile over time. Forever, it seemed, he had been pushed around, belittled, and forced to endure the relentless grind of bureaucracy for reasons as absurd as they were random. It had been dawning on society for a while, but the arrival of the gigantic sprouting tumour had finally blossomed a shared dementia amongst humanity that turned sense upside down. There were no rules anymore, nor were there facts to be proved. It was just one long line of madness that, if you didn't join, you were corrupted by in other ways.

Ronald's mind had found its fix, its core. He had done well to hold off the grinding sense of unreality with his own ideology of rules and regulations. But now that the cosy, familiar home of the council office had been taken from him, it had finally snapped and allowed itself to be moulded into a different, more left-field vision.

And so, leaving his house for the last time, Ronald Pile felt calm. Happy even. He had a purpose again, a mission in life. All the plates that he had spent his life spinning and making sure didn't fall and crack were now shards on the ground, and he was free to spin his own crockery. While the air wasn't fresh, and the clouds in the sky provided a thick gloom across West Crumb, keeping it in perpetual dusk, it was sunny in Ronald's world.

He walked down his street, waving at the last remnants of humanity who were not in the thrall of the Fleshberg. It was curious to observe how each little capsule of these rebels existed. Some were in a haze of drink and drugs, others valiantly fighting off the cultists who had come to collect them. Then, there were those that had simply given in to misery.

But not Ronald Pile, no sir. He had things to do now. As one West Crumb resident grasped at him and begged for help, he made his apologies with a skip in his step and a chuckle in his mood.

"Sorry, friend, I've got work to do," he said, as the fanatics pulled the woman away and into a waiting van.

He had a list and, like the festive fellow himself, he had checked it twice. Only with Ronald's list, there was no naughty or nice. No, his gift was all for the Fleshberg, and the horrid blight it had enveloped not just West Crumb in, but the world.

As he rounded corner after corner, he finally got to where he was heading. West Crumb High Street, home to the Fleshberg Fanatics.

Huge swathes of humanity all in awe of the thing that protruded above them all.

The Pillar.

The tower that Ronald would soon topple.

Yes, he thought, today would be a good day.

28

In terms of awkward scenarios, Laura's current position ranked quite high in her life. Sure, there had been the times where she had tucked her top into her pants by accident, or been caught between two friends as they broke up. But as she sat in her extravagant tent, wondering what her next step was, she tried her best not to meet the gaze of the fanatics standing there, staring.

It was as if she was holding court to an audience she didn't expect. Laura wasn't one for being the centre of attention, so as the eerie silence slithered through the air, she performed a variety of facial expressions as she considered what to say.

As it was, she didn't need to say anything.

"Can we get you anything?" a bespectacled man said.

"Err... a drink would be nice?"

The crowd murmured amongst themselves.

"Tea?" a short woman said.

"I prefer coffee."

Suddenly, the crowd burst into a hive of activity. Bodies seemed to swarm in and out of the mass in front of Laura, and before long a steaming hot brew was delivered to her.

It was actually quite good.

Maybe it was the caffeine that then kicked in, but Laura decided to be proactive about this whole weirdness.

"Why are you all staring at me?"

Jaws dropped and words were stammered, but eventually another short woman with red hair stepped forward.

"Kevin says you're important."

"Really?"

"Oh yes. To…"

The short redhead soon found an elbow in her ribs, and she sank into the crowd.

Laura thought about this, and then rolled her eyes as a theory made itself known.

"Is this 'cause he fancies me?"

The crowd muttered again.

"It makes sense. He becomes the head of some sort of… and do excuse the term here… but some sort of cult, and so he thinks by making me a goddess I'll be so grateful that… well, I presume that's the case?"

Nobody answered directly, but their shifting about suggested this was along the right lines.

"Thought so. Well if he thinks worshipping me is going to make me sleep with him, he's off by a long shot."

Laura sipped her coffee and got up to stretch.

"Besides, he'd need a serious shower first," she said. "And a burger."

Despite her direct approach, the crowd still stood there, awaiting her next proclamation to them. Honestly, it made Laura feel ever so slightly hacked off.

"What are you all waiting for?"

Again, the majority of folk there became slack-jawed.

"What do you expect me to do? A song and dance?"

"Kevin didn't really say," a tall man with long hair said.

"What did he say?"

"He said you'd come," another man said, prompting the crowd to nod and agree.

"And how did he know that?"

"Well, why else are you here?"

This question gave Laura pause. In her own mind, she and Joey had ventured down into the commune to find out what was going on first-hand. Now, though, she wondered why they would do such a thing, given they already knew the majority here were mental. Why hadn't they just stayed at home, and waited out whatever came next?

"You were drawn here," the short woman without red hair said, "just like us."

This seemed to please everyone. It was as if any sort of piercing of the whys and whatnots of their new lives would cause their whole psyche to collapse. Having a reason made all the doubt go away, naturally.

Not that that helped Laura.

"Look, I don't know what's going on… maybe that's why I'm here. Curiosity and all…"

"It killed the cat."

Kevin's arrival caught the crowd's attention, and provoked much laughter among them. Laura thought they were easily pleased. Nevertheless, he had returned.

Without Joey.

"Kevin, tell them I'm not a god," Laura said.

"You're not a god."

"Thank you."

"But you will meet one."

Laura didn't know what to say.

"I touched it, you know. The Fleshberg. And I saw it. Everything. And it was glorious."

"So that's why you look like shit?"

"Would you wash off the touch of something more than you?"

223

"If it smelt like that, yes," Laura said. "And when did you last eat for God's sake?"

"I don't do *anything* for 'His' sake anymore. He doesn't even compare to… It."

"What, you're now praying to a killer clown?"

Kevin laughed. "You mock, Laura, but you'll see."

"Right. Good. Now moving on, where's Joey?"

Kevin didn't answer. He just smiled.

Laura didn't like it.

"Kevin, where's Joey?"

Instead of answering, Kevin just allowed himself to sink into the crowd, out of sight.

"Kevin! You prick! Where's Joey?!"

"I think he showed him," the bespectacled man said.

Which was what Laura was afraid of.

-

As Laura was forced to hold court, Ronald was weaving his way through. True, to get to where he needed to go he could have gone the long route, but his mission to blow up the Fleshberg needed to be performed as soon as possible. For the sake of all that was living, he needed to enter the belly of the beast in order to kill it.

Or something like that. Even he admitted to himself that his thoughts were running away from him. He felt giddy, like a child doing something they know is wrong. He even made sure to play nice with the fanatics that he pushed his way through, recognising a few faces and giving a hearty greeting.

"Hello, Ronald," Nobby, an old drinking buddy, said. "Come to join us?"

"Not right now, Nobs. I've got something very important to do."

"Don't we all, mate," Nobby said, gesturing to the veiny pillar. "Hopefully it's coming soon."

"Oh yes," Ronald said. "It'll be soon."

Slinking away from Nobby, Ronald did his best to navigate his way in the direction of the council offices. There, he'd find everything he'd need to follow through his plan, and then everything would be OK.

Everything would be normal again.

Which made the presence of Moira slightly jarring.

Yes, she represented the old normality that Ronald lived with, but seeing her now, dressed barely in a nightie and covered in muck, it made him think of how the Fleshberg had violated West Crumb.

"What are you doing here?" she said.

"I... I'm doing something."

"What?"

Ronald struggled to answer. Suddenly, all his glee and confidence had been sapped and he was once more under the spell of his once darling wife.

"Have you come to see the Fleshberg?"

"In a manner of speaking."

"Oh good! I hoped you would eventually. We're going to see it soon."

"Really?"

"Oh yes. In a few hours or so. I'm very excited."

Moira grabbed Ronald's hands when she said this, and for a moment he flashed back to their wedding day, and all the other days where they had looked into each other's eyes and giggled at the love they had for each other.

That was another time. A better time.

Time the Fleshberg had taken away from him.

"I… must do something first. At the office," he said.

"Work? Now, Ronald? Can't it wait?"

"Oh, it won't take long."

Moira let go and, to Ronald's mind looked suspicious. She had known him better than he knew himself, and now he wondered if that was because she had some sort of psychic power. Or maybe the Fleshberg had given her psychic powers?

He didn't even believe in psychics, but his dealings with the Fleshberg and The Bureau had made a lot of things seem normal these days.

"I'll be back," he said. "Don't worry."

There was a pause, but soon Moira was beaming at him again.

"Well before you go, there's someone I'd like you to meet."

Moira grabbed Ronald's hand again, and almost dragged him through the crowd. Luckily, it was in the direction he wanted to go, and Moira was much better at parting a path than he was.

Unfortunately, she didn't pull him toward the council offices. She brought him to a big tent.

Where a young girl was calling somebody a prick.

"This is Laura," Moira said. "She's special."

Ronald and Laura looked at each other, and instantly realised the same thing.

They were the sane ones in a sea of nutters.

29

As Moira made the introductions, Laura did her best to smile, nod, and wish the mad woman would go away as soon as possible. She didn't care about this new man who had appeared, she just wanted to go inside her tent, drink heavily, and hope Joey was OK.

Then again, this 'Ronald' didn't look like them. For one, he looked like he had showered in the past week. Second, he looked as freaked out as she was.

Once Moira left Ronald standing there, herself vanishing into the crowd, Laura joined the fanatics in taking in his presence.

"Um, hello," he said.

Laura saw that the fanatics weren't as interested in his company as they were in hers.

"Do you talk, or are you…"

"I'm not one of them," Laura said.

"She's special," someone in the crowd said.

"Shut up."

Her mood well and truly riled up, Laura snapped back into her plan and headed inside the tent. She grabbed the zippers and swiftly pulled them up so that she didn't have to look at the insane rabble around her anymore.

Before she fully closed the flap, she looked at Ronald.

"Need a drink?"

"Um, well..."

"Yes, no, or fuck off."

"Yes it is, then."

Once Ronald had stumbled his way inside, he looked at the nice arrangement inside the tent. Either this girl had fine taste in decoration, or something weird was going on.

He knew that more than likely it was the latter.

"Beer?"

"I'm more of a whisky man."

Laura shrugged, and threw the can to Ronald.

"If I may, what are you doing here?"

"I could ask you the same thing."

"I'm on my way to the council offices."

"You work for the council... wait, didn't I see you on TV?"

Ronald hoped not.

"You were the idiot who announced the end of the world, weren't you?"

"I'd rather not talk about that."

"I can't imagine why. Tell me, how's that working for you?"

"Look... I have to get to the council offices..."

"You said that," Laura said, cracking open a can with a fizz. "Why?"

"I'm going to blow up the Fleshberg."

Laura nearly spat out her beer.

There was a pause between them, as both wondered if Ronald's statement had been heard by the crowds outside. He could see their shadows still lurking around, but no worrying movement was made.

"You're going to what?"

Ronald collected himself and thought over his words.

"I'm going to do the right thing," he said with a wink.

Laura nodded slowly.

"And how do you plan to do that?"

"Um, I just said how."

"Yeah, but how will you do *that*?"

"Oh. I see. Well, I work for the horticulture area of the council. Parks and such. And we have a lot of, well, fertiliser about the place. For gardeners."

"Or terrorists."

"I can assure you, young lady, we do not give fertiliser to terrorists."

"And yet, here you are…"

Laura smiled as she saw Ronald contemplate his new role in life.

"I suppose so."

"How the Hell do you think you'll manage to get away with it? You've seen how they all are out there. How they act. They're like a hive."

"Well, bees are easily distracted," he said, with a certain air of cockiness.

It didn't impress.

"OK I don't know. But I suppose a distraction would be a good plan."

"It would be a better plan than composting the whole place," Laura said. "Lucky for you, I know the queen bee."

"I thought that analogy wasn't working anymore?"

"Me, you tit."

Ronald was now very confused.

"They seem to worship me, so I'll distract them while you… do what you need to do."

"Which firstly is to get to the council offices."

"Fine," Laura said, knocking back her beer and getting up. "You ready?"

"Really? Now?"

232

"Of course now! When else do you want to do it? Next week?"

Ronald got up, smiled and nodded.

"Ready!"

With that, Laura walked over, opened the tent, and took in the expectant faces before her. She wondered how she could use her influence to get Ronald safe passage to the council offices to make his bomb, and finally end this whole thing once and for all.

In the moment, however, she failed to come up with a plan even vaguely cunning, so instead went with the horribly obvious.

"I command you all to help this man get to the council offices," she said.

Ronald wasn't sure it would work.

But after a bit of confused muttering, the crowd agreed.

And Ronald Pile was swiftly escorted to where he needed to go.

Laura just hoped they wouldn't end up feeding him to Kevin instead.

-

As it was, Kevin remained none the wiser of Ronald's intentions.

The crowd of fanatics were blasé about it, even if they *had* heard about his bomb plot. Instead, they casually walked him through the commune, giving him a jolly wave as he broke off from them and into the West Crumb Council building.

It was just how he had left it – cold, empty, and lifeless. No bored girls greeted him at reception; no far-too-chipper ladies asked if he needed help.

Just an empty building, gutted of everything it once had.

While it was spooky walking through the once bustling halls, it was also kind of sad. This had been the place Ronald had called work for the past few decades, and now it was just a shell, left to rot as everyone's priorities shifted from local governance to a giant tumour.

Thankfully, that sadness grew to an anger that fuelled Ronald further to go through with his plan.

He headed to the backyard, where most of the gardening supplies were held. Of course, it wasn't simply a case of walking in and taking what he needed. No, due to the nature of the materials – the nature being you could make a bloody bomb with them – Ronald needed a key. And only one person he knew had a key.

Ronald Pile.

So, pepped up by the memory of minor power he had, Ronald climbed the stairs and ventured toward his office. He'd hid the key in one of his drawers, and hoped that it hadn't been torn apart like everything else. Since he'd last been here, any sign of activity had been swept away completely. He sensed that The Bureau had returned, and decided a Scorched Earth policy was best in this scenario.

234

As he made his way to his old desk, old memories doing their best to haunt him, he reached for the drawer.

It opened, and greeted him with a picture of him and Moira.

For a moment, the old reality started to come back. The ghosts of the office became louder, more real, and Ronald was once again just another council drone looking after the local parks. The smell of fresh coffee and cold sandwiches wafted through the air, and he heard Moira say that they were visiting the in-laws that week. That Ronald had better bring a bottle, just in case.

Ronald Pile was almost seeing his life flash before his eyes, and it allowed him a moment to shed a tear and pine for yesterday.

But that, of course, was yesterday. When there was no Fleshberg. No disgusting Pillar. No shared hysteria or madness.

All that was already a memory. As much as Ronald could try to chase it, it would always outrun him.

Instead, the ghosts faded, the smells vanished, and the dull void around him returned.

And behind the picture, was the key.

Now, I could tell you all about what Ronald got, how he used it, and how it ultimately made a bomb, but that would be very irresponsible. Suffice to say - when Ronald Pile left the West Crumb Council offices, in his backpack he had a device that would spread the Fleshberg all across West Crumb.

He just needed to get close enough to do it.

30

As if finely tuned into her own self, the weather began to shift into a place as dark as Laura's mood. Truly, she felt miserable, pissed off, and very much alone.

It, in her own thoughts, sucked quite the balls.

She never really allowed herself to be taken by her own emotions. Like many of her generation, these were unnecessary things that distracted from the important things in life, like social media and alcohol. Right now, sitting in a tent decorated like a bloody shrine, surrounded by the shadows of weirdoes who revered her, Laura actually felt like crying.

It wasn't a pleasant feeling, so she did her best to swallow it back down again.

Then she thought of Joey, and it happened.

It would have been cathartic, perhaps. The release she needed in order to focus and become more confident and proactive in whatever she had planned next. It should have been, ironically, a positive experience.

However, one of the fanatics outside heard her sobs, and asked if she was OK.

The very fact that in her most vulnerable moment, Laura was still being invaded by idiots who sat around in their own muck and

worshipped a giant blob that had vomited up grotesque strings? Well…
she went straight from being sad to being insanely pissed off.

And now she was angry, she was ready to do something about
it.

Laura unzipped the tent and was greeted by the dumb, smiling
faces of Kevin's little Fleshberg cult. They didn't say anything, but
they looked ready to fall on their knees and bow to her if she said the
right thing.

What she actually said was definitely not that thing.

"I need a piss."

The smiles faded, and confusion once again took control of the
fanatics. Laura wondered at that moment if upon entering the Fleshberg
cult, one had to have their brains scooped out and replaced by jelly. The
way they all stumbled into what to do in the face of Laura's
proclamation was nothing short of disturbing in its stupidity.

"Well? Where's the toilet?"

"I don't think we have one," a bald man said.

"You don't have a toilet? Where do you shit?"

More dumb faces.

"Do you shit?"

"We… well, we just go on the ground."

Laura looked down, and noticed that the rugs and covers that hid the swirling Fleshberg veins underneath were covered in a variety of stains it was best not to ask about.

"So you expect me to just squat and go?"

The crowd answered in shrugs and awkward glances.

"Fuck that," Laura said. "Take me to the nearest pub."

"Um, we can't," a tall lady said.

"You can't take me to the pub? You do know what a pub is, don't you? Or have you all completely lost your minds?"

"Of course we know what a pub is," a bearded man said. "We just…"

"Just what?"

"We can't take you there."

"Why not?"

"Because… it's nearly time."

Laura didn't like the sound of this.

"Time for what?"

Once again, the crowd went mild.

"Oi! Your revered lady here wants to know what it is time for?"

Still no one spoke. It was as if a big secret had been awkwardly revealed, and now they were trying to gaslight their way out of it.

"OK. I'll tell you what it *is* time for," Laura said. "It's time for me to leave."

As she got up and out the tent, the crowd suddenly enclosed itself around her. Try as she might, Laura couldn't squeeze past the sheer amount of human disaster that stood around her. She was tempted to start throwing fists, but looking at the faces of the people, she realised they were about as happy doing this as she was having to fight through it all.

"Please," one girl said, "just... just calm down."

"Calm down? Why should I calm down? What the Hell is happening here? What are you all doing? What the *fuck* is that?"

Laura pointed at the Pillar, writhing thickly and slowly, oblivious to any and all drama.

Of course, no one answered.

"Come on! You've been hoisting people up there for the last few days, so what is it?"

"It's... it's a pillar."

"I know it's a bloody pillar, you twat. Where does it go?"

The eyes of the crowd seemed to burst into life, as they widened and glazed over in rapture.

Laura knew there was no more sense to be carved out, so she charged forward.

And bounced straight off a fairly corpulent lady.

As Laura seethed in her mildly apologetic face, there was a murmuring elsewhere. She turned, expecting to see Kevin again in all his rotten glory, but instead was greeted by a smiling woman. Laura wondered if she was someone from one of her classes, being so young and, more importantly, not dressed in smelly rags. It was like seeing someone from the past pop through a portal.

"It's time," she said.

A collective silence fell upon the crowd.

"Time for what," Laura said.

"Your destiny."

"Care to share what that is?"

Laura didn't like the way the girl smiled.

"You're the chosen one."

While the crowd expected Laura to take this information with the glory it suggested, she instead slumped her shoulders and sighed.

"You got to be fucking kidding me."

-

With his backpack safely hoisted over his shoulders and ready to go, Ronald Pile re-entered the Fleshberg commune.

It was time to unleash his mission.

He knew he probably should be more careful, with the contents of the bomb in his pack swimming about dangerously as he moved. But he was confident he had taped it up securely so that any dangerous chemicals wouldn't spill out until the time was right. Or something like that.

Ronald wasn't really a bomb expert. He just knew that once he flipped the switch, things would start cooking.

Literally.

The only issue now was how to get to the Fleshberg. All the manholes leading to the sewers were patrolled by fanatics, looking far more sanitary than the others. He guessed it wouldn't be a case of simply walking over to them and asking politely if he could scoot on down, so he could blow up the violation below.

Instead, he tried to remember the blueprints of the town. Whether there were any other entry points to the sewers originating in nearby streams or outlets.

As Ronald considered this, he felt someone come close.

"You came back!"

"Moira," Ronald said, eyes darting around in shock. "You're naked."

"Well I don't want to get my clothes dirty."

"Dirty?"

"Yes. We're going to see the Fleshberg."

Ronald began to smile.

"Can I come," he said.

"Don't be silly, Ronald. Of course you can! That's why I came to get you. Did you want to…?"

Moira was looking over Ronald, but he gave an awkward laugh and made sure the backpack was securely about his person.

"I think I'll keep my clothes on, my dear."

"Are you sure? We are going into a sewer."

"Personal preference."

"You always did like to go against the grain, Ronald," Moira said, smiling lovingly at him and taking him by the end.

As his wife escorted him to the nearest open manhole, Ronald took in other fanatics in various states of undress. They all gossiped between them in excited tones, like children about to go on a field trip. Even those manning the entry seemed giddy.

"You're so lucky," one said to Ronald as Moira began to descend.

"You have no idea."

Ronald took his first steps onto the ladder, and eased his way below West Crumb. Once his feet hit the wet slime below, the sheer intensity of the smell invaded his nostrils and threatened to bring up any remaining food he had in his stomach.

With a firm swallow and determined constitution, Ronald collected himself and saw Moira ahead of him, in a small queue of people.

"Come on, Ronald. Keep up."

Ronald hurried over to his wife, and walked alongside her as they navigated the tunnels of the sewer. It wasn't as large as he expected, but was definitely as horrid. The walls seemed to ooze around him, and he felt he'd catch something if he even went near anything down here.

Not that any of that really mattered, as in a short moment the whole place would be opened up to the street above.

One thing did bother Ronald though. He expected the dirt, and he expected the slime and disgust, but he also expected rats. In his tenure at West Crumb Council, rats had been a constant problem, and always dwelled deep below the town. Now he was down here, though, there was nothing. Not a screech or a squeal. The only sign of life were the fanatics he slowly marched in line with.

And, of course, the veins.

It wasn't until he turned a corner that they really began to stand out; snaking along the walls and pulsating with whatever was inside of them. Some were thin and delicate, but there were huge, thick trunks of fleshy tentacles that slithered along the wall.

"Ronald, stop looking at the sewer and come along," Moira said.

"My dear, don't you think all of this is… horrible?"

"Horrible?"

"Yes, horrible. I mean, look at us. We're in a sewer! There are horrid, meaty snakes all around us, climbing the walls and... whatnot."

"Ronald, you do make a fuss..."

"Of course I'm making a fuss! Don't you see?"

"Quite frankly, no. I do not. Now come on, I think we're nearly there."

As they approached a corner, Ronald lost control of his senses and was hit by the smell again. This was worse, though. It was a rancid aroma that he'd never come across before. Well, tell a lie, part of his memory told him he had come across it before, but very rarely.

If he'd taken notice of the reddening of the water, and chunks of debris, he may have put the equation together.

As it was, he instead fell into awe at the sight of the Fleshberg.

To very little surprise, it was exactly as it looked on the films he had seen. Its intense mass blocked the route through the sewer, and in the dim light provided it sparkled with a creamy pink colour, soaked in a thick gloss. The tendrils popped out of it like eyes on a potato, flailing out toward the walls and broken architecture of the sewer.

And once he had taken this all in, Ronald saw the horror of his fate.

The fanatics in front of him and Moira were walking into the Fleshberg, and being absorbed. They didn't seem in pain, or even upset about the whole experience, but it didn't look pleasant. Once they touched the fleshy mass, it sucked them in and slowly made them break apart under the surface of what seemed like its skin.

Seeing a person's smile widen thanks to their lips dissolving made Ronald want to vomit.

Unfortunately, this made him lose focus. As Moira grabbed his hand and pulled him closer for their turn, he forgot about the bomb in his backpack. He needed to flick a switch to activate it, so that the chemicals would heat up, mix, and cause one Hell of a blast.

As it hit him, he flung the backpack off one arm.

His other arm was being held by Moira.

"Oh, Ronald. It's time," she said.

"Moira, let go."

"This is so exciting."

"Moira, please."

Soon enough, the naked body of Ronald's wife Moira was stuck to the Fleshberg, and slowly eaten by it. As she sunk in, Ronald tried to wrestle his hand from his grip in order to take off the backpack and reach inside.

But she was too strong. She had always been too strong. It had been cute, back in the day, the way she could easily hold onto him, never letting go.

Now Ronald was panicking, the grip was a curse. Soon enough, Moira had been taken in by the Fleshberg, and pulled Ronald along with her.

Once his hand was inside, he felt his skin tingle and fizz. It didn't hurt, but it didn't relent either. No matter how hard he pulled, he couldn't get his wrist out. Or his arm. Before Ronald knew it, he was contorting his body, trying to reach around and unzip the backpack.

As he fumbled in vain, Ronald was drawn deeper and deeper into the Fleshberg, until his face grimaced in frustrated agony before dissolving into nothingness.

Along with his backpack.

Along with his bomb.

And that was the end of Ronald Pile.

31

Much like most things in modern life, it was useless to struggle against what was happening. Those who believe in fate, destiny, and the overall belief in an unfluctuating narrative would agree that to try and go against it is to invite futility in your life. This is just the way life goes, accept it and move on.

The thing is, when said destiny involves being led to a pillar made out of thousands of squirming, worm-like veins, it all seems a bit off. Lives are meant to be, at their roots, simple. You're born, you live, you die. Beginning, middle, end.

Nowhere in that narrative does it mention a giant ball of flesh giving birth to a trunk stretching into the sky.

Now she was closer to the Pillar, Laura could see in more horrible detail the mass of tentacles that made up its body. It tangled itself again and again, until it was impossible to break through the goliath trunk.

As for the height? Imagine standing at the base of a skyscraper. One that towered for more storeys than you can possibly imagine. Imagine how much that dwarfs you, makes you feel sick from the sheer scale.

That's what Laura felt looking up from the base of the Pillar. Here, she saw that the clouds didn't signal the end of it. The Fleshberg

Pillar stretched beyond the clouds and into the dark sky above, maybe even space.

Hell, as far as she knew, maybe it was infinite. It wouldn't surprise Laura at this stage.

The young woman who led her here had since fallen back amongst the rabble that had gathered to watch the spectacle. Laura herself was under no illusions about what was going to happen. If she had time to digest everything, she would think of how it probably was always going to lead to this.

Part of her hoped that Joey had climbed it as well.

But she also knew better.

"Excited?"

Laura smelt Kevin, so didn't need to acknowledge him.

"You're going on a great journey, Laura."

"Why don't you join me?"

Kevin laughed. It actually sounded genuine, like he was human. The conspiracy theorist she met in the pub way back when.

Then he spoke, and his voice oozed from between the rot in his mouth.

"I wish I could. I do. But I am needed here, at the base. It is not for me to go and embrace It."

"The killer clown."

"Laura, you're thinking too binary."

"I'm thinking of a horror movie villain," she said, wishing she'd said book instead.

"What you're about to experience is more than just… this," Kevin said, gesturing to something, or maybe everything. "It's more than flesh and bone, presence and thought. It's something *far* more. *Far greater.*"

"You know how clichéd you sound? Like, did this 'It' give you an idiot's guide to being a cult leader?"

"I don't know why you continue to mock me, when I'm giving you the gift of greatness."

"Because you're a dickhead, Kevin. I thought you were a dickhead when I first met you. I'll admit, you surprised me though. Because when I first thought you were a dickhead, I thought there's no way on this planet that you could excel further at being a dickhead. And yet, here you are, brilliantly blasting through the realms of what we thought a dickhead was. And maybe you're right? Maybe what I'll see up there will be something unlike I've ever known. Maybe it's the greatest dickhead in the history of all dickheads, turning dickheads into something we never imagined."

Kevin looked at Laura, no longer enjoying the moment.

"Please don't ruin this for me," he said.

"You know, I'm dreadfully sorry. I didn't consider how important this was for you."

"Please stop."

"No, Kevin. I'm being sincere. I've always wanted to climb an ugly, disgusting mass of veins into a sky leading into an endless void. Why, you're my Prince Fucking Charming, helping me realise my dreams and making them come true."

With the crowd silent around them, Laura and Kevin looked at each other. For a moment, it actually felt normal. A real confrontation between two young people.

Then, Kevin said, "just climb the fucking thing."

And without any other options, Laura put her hand on the pillar, and felt the tendrils curl around it.

There was no going back now.

-

He didn't really deserve the abuse.

After all, he'd been chosen. Out of the entire group who had gone down to see the Fleshberg, he was the one that was still alive. While the others had been absorbed to help it grow, help it live, it had spared Kevin.

Not only that, it had shown him visions.

He had seen things that made his head hurt. Colours outside human perception. Shapes that defied known physics. Forget the idea of aliens; the beings he saw weren't made of flesh and bone. Kevin didn't even know if they were beings, or just consciousness and thought in some aspect of physical form.

At that moment, he knew what he had to do. He had to tell everyone, spread the word and bring them all here. The Fleshberg already had some influence in that, but he could do more.

In theory he could, anyway.

Kevin would be the first to admit he wasn't good at rounding people up to his beliefs. Luckily, the Fleshberg helped him with Aaron Stone. Aaron had been far more comfortable promoting the Fleshberg, making an attraction for people to not just see, but to believe in.

As the Pillar grew, so did Kevin's community. His believers became more and more devout, with those that lost belief being sacrificed for the betterment of the Fleshberg.

Aaron included.

Throughout this growth, both physically and spiritually, Kevin kept in mind the idea that the Fleshberg had given him. The plan to help the creator come to our world and bring us to the next stage of our collective evolution.

He had to send an emissary of true glory. A light amongst the darkness that was humanity.

It was Laura. It had always been Laura.

She personified the greatness in life to Kevin. She was beautiful. She was funny. Most importantly, she was defiant. Strong. A warrior woman who did not accept the norm, the roles that life would

253

try to hoist upon her. She was the perfect person to bring about the new age, the new dawn. She was Kevin's one true angel. The first of the chosen. The *only* one chosen.

And now she was heading toward It. She would see what Kevin had only seen in dreams and moments of possessed clarity.

He wasn't jealous.

He just wished he could have been with her beforehand.

-

During the climb up the Pillar, time lost all meaning.

Laura wasn't so much ascending, as she was being pulled up by the tentacles making up the fleshy column. Each time her hand or foot was freed, and she reached for her next movement, one would become loose from the mass and help her with her next step.

She had tried allowing herself to slip, to fall away and end this whole charade. But the pillar kept a firm grip on her. Like she had seen before, a couple of appendages had snaked itself in the loops of her jeans and around her waist. Even if she did let go, she'd only hang there limply, enjoying the view the great height afforded her.

And the view was quite something. As Laura stopped to catch her breath, she looked around to see that West Crumb was nothing more than a map. A tableau where only the odd building stood out and looked vaguely familiar among the shades and shapes. The people were now gone, invisible in the sheer scope of the height she was at.

Looking up, Laura saw how close she was to the end.

254

Or something resembling an end.

She wasn't sure when she had passed the clouds, but theorised that she had definitely done so recently. She was too high up to be at the point she had seen others ascend. But she was still climbing, still heading toward a huge swathe of darkness. It was like staring into space, but the whole atmosphere and environment didn't feel like the edge of the Earth. She still felt relatively close, comfortable even. It felt no different than being up a rather large hill.

Then, as Laura took her next steps, she felt the tendrils loosen around her. For a moment, she was free, able to move of her own will.

So she decided to end it. She decided to fall.

And Laura did fall.

Up, into a void severed by colourful fissions and bleeding stars.

32

Kevin had never really liked his followers.

While those of fragile ego often crave leadership, he was finding that it was like a wish from a monkey's paw. A false promise that wasn't as good as it should be.

It was their moaning he couldn't stand. The constant whinging and whining that nothing was happening. That they weren't yet experiencing the glory they had been promised.

It made him sick.

He had told them they needed to be patient. He told them that things were happening as expected, and that their new dawn was fast approaching. But unlike the other things, he didn't have a timeline. He didn't know when It would come and bless them. When Laura would return as their new queen.

And it had only been a day since she made the climb. What did they expect to happen?

"Something more than nothing," Olivia, one of Kevin's most loyal followers, said.

"Oh shut up."

"Wish I could, but let's be honest, they're starting to crack."

This wasn't what Kevin wanted to hear. If his followers – or rather, the Fleshberg's followers – were beginning to crack, this didn't mean they were going crazy. After all, they already were crazy, if one were to look at them in a normal society.

No, to go crazy in Kevin's world was to go sane again.

It meant realising that there was no great, mystical being beyond. That there was only a man behind the curtain.

And they would think that man was Kevin.

"You still believe?" he said.

"I mean..."

"Olivia..."

"Belief is a flexible thing, Kevin. It's easily manipulated."

"You think I'm manipulating them?"

"I'm saying they're fickle. They need a sign."

"Now I know how Jesus felt..."

Kevin emerged from the shop he had converted into his own private sanctuary, and looked out upon the crowds of people that were nervously looking up the Pillar. As soon as one saw him, they all turned to Kevin and barked questions in one, tangled voice. They asked when It was coming, why It had not come yet, and if Laura had died.

Kevin smiled, did his best to placate them, and then tried to think what to do next. The sacrifices had worn off, the Fleshberg no longer consuming people into itself. And sending more people to climb was now impossible given the pillar had stopped supporting them, and was coated in a slippery sheen.

Instead, Kevin fell back on old platitudes.

"Good things come to those who wait."

It didn't work.

He soon heard the first dissenting voice. A young man —
because they always moaned first – declaring the whole thing to be
rubbish and a "load of bollocks". Another person then spoke up, and
another. Soon, the lone voices were gathering into one booming roar,
and Kevin could feel his grip on his followers loosen.

More than anything, he needed a sign.

He got one.

Via text.

As his phone pinged, he took it out of his pocket almost
casually. It was a relic of the past, and he hadn't exactly been popular
beforehand. All his friends were now gone, absorbed by the Fleshberg
or up the Pillar, into the other side.

Which made the notification make some sort of twisted sense.

"I have a message," he said.

The crowd calmed a bit. There were still angry faces full of
disappointment and feelings of deception, but they were in too deep
now. One last chance for Kevin to redeem himself was fair.

"It's from Laura."

"The chosen one?" someone said.

"No, another Laura," Olivia said, before being silenced by Kevin.

He opened up his phone, and read the text.

"What does it say?"

"Where is she?"

"Does this mean she's alive?"

Kevin was sweating. His stomach was lurching in all manner of motions that didn't sit well at all. For a moment, he felt like he was going to faint.

Olivia managed to steady him, and he read the text to the crowd.

"It says, PREPARE YOURSELF."

The crowd murmured between themselves, torn between excitement and confusion.

Kevin neglected to tell them the added MOTHERFUCKER to the message.

It didn't seem right to mention.

-

Somewhere outside the planet, outside reality, a series of monitors were tuned into West Crumb and other assorted locations on Earth. They showed all sorts of scenes – panic, acceptance, complete obliviousness.

And watching this all unfold were a group of people in labcoats and suits.

Including Grounding Agent March Sunday.

"Anything happening yet?"

Sunday turned to face Agent Keating, armed with a bag of popcorn and an impatient manner.

"Not yet."

"But it's going to happen?"

Agent Sunday looked at their device.

"99.9% recurring."

"So…"

"Yes, P847 will end soon."

Agent Keating nodded, and continued chewing on his popcorn. He had never seen an apocalypse before, and was excited at the prospect.

"What exactly will happen," he said. "Like, will there be explosions? Rivers of blood? Or will it just…"

He snapped his fingers.

Agent Sunday glared at him.

"It always depends on the scenario."

Agent Keating nodded, finished off his popcorn, and took his leave.

For Agent Sunday, this had happened many times before. These things always did. No matter the time, the place, or the circumstance, eventually an end would come and an existence would cease to be. This particular end had happened a few times on their watch; the small town of West Crumb playing host to a being planted by an Eldritch, that soon caused equal parts hysteria and doom. Sometimes it would happen quickly, sometimes it would not happen at all.

But eventually, when it did happen, it always happened the same way.

The Violation would return, and it would not be pretty.

Maybe Agent Keating would get his rivers of blood. Maybe he'd just get a standard massacre. Maybe, it would just be a general ripping apart of the laws of physics. But, once the Violation came back, it would always result in the end.

For a moment, Agent Sunday thought back to Ronald Pile and his actions during this particular timeline. Not only had he played an intriguing part with Aaron Stone, but he had also had a fleeting moment with the Violation themselves.

Of course, he didn't know she was the Violation. As far as Ronald Pile knew, she was just a very angry student in a tent.

The thought prompted one of the rare occasions where Agent Sunday gave a slight chuckle.

Grounding Agents had an interesting sense of humour.

262

33

The messages had continued for a few more days. Each time, they were more threatening and mocking than the last.

It made Kevin very nervous.

He started to doubt himself, doubt the whole damned thing. Maybe he'd made a mistake, misinterpreted the visions he had been given.

Maybe, just maybe, he was an idiot after all.

That's what Laura had told him in the messages. She had not held back with her opinion of Kevin and his little power trip. Sure, she had belittled him before climbing toward It, but now? It was like she was reaching inside his head and squeezing every insecurity and pain that he had.

Of course, he didn't tell his followers this. Instead, he promised the forthcoming new dawn. Laura was coming back, he told them, and everything would change for the better.

Soon enough, the messages stopped. The last one Kevin received was simple in its threat.

IT'S TIME.

After this, Kevin and his followers noticed that the Pillar began to break down. The tendrils dried up and broke off, the once pulsating veins below the rugs and carpet now crunched in a sad, desiccated death.

Even the Fleshberg, once mighty and the progenitor of a new life, began to wither and collapse inwardly.

The Pillar was still firm, and Kevin remained calm in the face of this development. On this, the final day, he stepped out in front of his followers, smiled widely, and opened his arms.

"My friends, it is time."

"You said that last time," someone said.

"I know… but this time it really is. Look up, everyone, and witness the dawn of a new beginning."

"He said that too," the same someone said.

Kevin ignored them.

-

It was probably best.

As it *was* time, the new beginning *was* due.

For climbing the pillar beyond this dimension, was Laura.

Not the same Laura who had climbed into the void from West Crumb, though. This was a very different girl to the one that had first arrived in this realm. She was no longer a university student. She was no longer a woman who enjoyed a drink with her best friend. She had changed. She was different.

And she was very, very angry.

Worst of all for those waiting, she wasn't alone.

Oli Jacobs is a bearded chap who enjoys spinning a yarn or two. While now a hermit, he has been rumoured to be seen drinking cocktails and enjoying chicken in the wilds of Southampton. If seen, please approach gently as he has severe anxiety and may cry.

As well as writing this book, Oli is also a Book Bloggers Novel of the Year finalist (2021 – Wilthaven), and had stories featured by author Dane Cobain, and Bag of Bones Press.

As always, he hopes you enjoy.

Check out his writing at:

https://olijbooks.wordpress.com/

Follow him on Twitter at:

https://twitter.com/OliJacobsAuthor

Printed in Great Britain
by Amazon

Other Oli Jacobs titles include:

The Filmic Cuts series

Sunshine & Lollipop

Luchador Monkey Crisis

Curse of the Ellipsis…

Title Pending

Suplex Sounds of the 70s

The Lament of the Silver Badger

The Mr Blank series

Wrapped Up In Nothing

Night Train

The Kirk Sandblaster Series

Space Adventurer

The Ice Pirates of Llurr

The Game of Yloria

TETRAGEDDON

Montague Santiago

Xlaar's World War

Protocol 9

Faces the End

Short stories featured in:

Flash Fear

Subject Verb Object

Bag of Bones – 206 Word Stories

Well, This Is Tense